MW01136730

MILES EVER AFTER

THE MILES HIGH CLUB

T L SWAN

ALSO BY TL SWAN

ACKNOWLEDGMENTS

There are not enough words to express my gratitude for this life I get to live.
To be able to write books for a living is a dream come true.
But not just any books, I get to write exactly what I want to, stories that I love.
To my wonderful team,
Kellie, Alina, and Lauren. Thank you for everything that you do for me,
You are so talented and so appreciated.
You keep me sane.
To my fabulous beta readers, you make me so much better.
My beautiful mum who reads everything I write and gives me never ending support.
My husband and three beautiful kids, thanks for putting up with my workaholic ways.
And to you, the best most supportive readers in the entire world.
Thank you for loving The Miles High Series as much as I do.
I'm so sad to be closing the door on this series, but as we know, when one door closes,
Another one opens.
So much to look forward to.
All my love,
Tee xoxo

GRATITUDE

The quality of being thankful;
readiness to show appreciation for, and to return kindness.

DEDICATION

I would like to dedicate this book to the alphabet.
For those twenty-six letters have changed my life.
Within those twenty-six letters, I found myself
and live my dream.
Next time you say the alphabet remember its power.
I do every day.

THE STOPOVER EPILOGUE

THE MILES HIGH CLUB

1

THE STOPOVER EPILOGUE

Emily

THE ELEVATOR DOORS open and I step out into the foyer. "Hi, Sammia." I smile as I walk through reception.

"Thank god you're here." She widens her eyes.

I giggle, I know that look.

"One of those days, is it?" I ask.

"You could say that."

"My husband is a grump."

"You're a good woman." Sammia smirks as she turns back to her computer. "He's in his office."

"Thanks." I head down the corridor. I've taken the afternoon off work and have come to check on Jameson, something is off.

I'm not sure what's going on with him at the moment but I can always gauge his stress levels by the way we have sex. The more stressed out he is, the rougher the sex.

We haven't made love for weeks and weeks and yet we fuck hard every day.

Then yesterday, he went for three runs, one in the morning, one when he got home and then another at 10 p.m. before he went to bed...so I think it's pretty safe to say, my husband is stressed.

But what else is new?

Jameson Miles is a ball of restless energy, the kind that can't be calmed with a run in Central Park, no matter how fast he goes.

I knock on his door. "Knock, knock."

"What is it?" he calls.

Jeez.

I smirk and open the door; I find him staring at his computer screen. "What do you want?" he asks without looking up.

"Human resources sent me up to see you, sir, I got caught watching porn on my work computer."

His eyes rise to meet mine and he stares at me for a beat. "Is that so?"

"Yes, sir."

His jaw clenches as his gaze drops to my toes and back up to my face and he runs his tongue over his teeth.

I'm not playing fair, I'm here for one reason and one reason only.

Desk-fuck my man.

I'm wearing my sexiest secretary outfit, the one that he loves. Gray skirt and silk blouse, complete with suspender belt and crotchless panties.

"And what were you watching?" he replies curtly.

"*Sucking the CEO's Cock*, sir."

His eyebrow rises, he picks up a remote and pushes the button, I hear the door click locked behind me.

4

"And why would you watch *Sucking the CEO's Cock*?" he asks, void of emotion.

"It's a fantasy that I haven't explored yet."

"Is that so?"

"I...." I pause for added effect. "I just always wondered what you'd taste like.... I know you're married but...." I shrug.

Why is being naughty so fun?

"But what?" he snaps.

"I was just wondering if there was any way I could suck you off, sir?"

He inhales sharply and sits back in his chair; we stare at each other. The air swirling between us.

I love this game.

"This is a media company, Emily. Not a brothel."

"Yes, sir, I know."

"If my wife ever found out."

"She won't." I lick my lips and my eyes drop to his crotch. "I swear to you on my life."

He stands and unzips his suit trousers. "Get on your fucking knees," he growls.

I drop to the floor as I try to keep myself from smiling, even now. Married to him for over a year, role-playing this is my favorite thing.

Perverted.

He walks over and pushes the hair back from my face as he looks down at me, his thumb swipes over my lips. "You be a good girl and show me what you think about."

I nod and open my mouth; he drags the tip of his cock over my tongue and I taste the pre-ejaculate as it smears across my tastebuds.

He hisses in approval. "I'm going to fuck your dirty little mouth, Emily."

Arousal thrums through me.

"And you are going to regret your misdemeanor." He grabs my hair in his hands aggressively. "Aren't you?"

"No, sir."

He raises an eyebrow. "Did you say no to me?"

I nod, butterflies dancing in my stomach, no matter how well I know this man or how much he loves me, there's always an edge of danger when I poke the bear.

I nod.

"Big mistake." He slides his cock so far down my throat that I gag, but that doesn't stop him. He pushes in deeper until my eyes water.

I pull off him with a cough.

He chuckles. "Don't bother coughing, wimp." He pushes himself into my mouth again and again, my hair is gripped in his two hands as he fucks my mouth.

Hard and unapologetic.

Just how I like it.

I imagine what we must look like, me on my knees in his office. Him...riding my mouth. Pumping me over and over to the sound of his labored breathing.

I feel him harden even further and I clench my legs together, he's going to come without me.

"Suck me," he growls. "Harder." His grip on my hair is near painful and next thing I know he pulls me to my feet and bends me over his desk, he lifts my skirt and hisses as he sees my suspenders and crotchless panties. "Fuck yeah."

He slams into me in one sharp movement as he pushes my face into the desk with an open hand on my cheek as he holds me still.

"Oh..." I whimper, completely taken over by the dominance of this man.

Perfection.

He rides me hard, and I see stars. His thick cock taking exactly what it needs from my body. The sound of my wet flesh sucking him in and I spiral out of control as a tidal wave of pleasure rolls over me.

He slams in once, twice...three times, and then holds himself deep as his body takes over. Releasing his pent-up emotions, coming hard deep inside my body.

We pant, trying to come back to earth, and he pulls me to my feet and kisses me tenderly.

So different to the way he just took me.

But that's us. A normal day.

The perfect contradiction.

He holds my face in his hands as he kisses me again. "Good afternoon, Mrs. Miles." He smiles darkly against my lips.

"You're a fucking deviant," I whisper.

He pulls down my skirt and rearranges my shirt. "And you're full of me, so I win."

He falls into his office chair and pulls me down onto his lap, he nuzzles his head into my breast and just sits for a while.

While I'm instantly sated and softened, I feel an undertone of anxiety from him. Uneasiness rolls over me, he is really wound up. I can still feel it within him, oozing from his soul.

I glance over and see a half-drunk glass of scotch on his desk and then look at the time on his computer: 1 p.m.

"Why are you day drinking?" I ask.

He sighs in an overexaggerated way. "Don't."

"Jameson. Don't *don't* me." I stand. "You are too stressed, this has got to stop."

"I'm fine, don't carry on and ruin it."

"Do you understand that we cannot try for a baby until you get this stress under control?"

"I do not have time for a vacation, Emily."

"Yes you do. I'm calling Tristan, he can come and fill in for you."

He rolls his eyes, unimpressed. "Did you come here to take me to lunch or what?"

"Don't change the subject," I snap, I pick up the glass of scotch and pour it down the sink. "I came here to suck your dick actually, no more day drinking." I tell him.

"Yes, Mom."

"Yes," I snap. "That is exactly right, I want to be a mother. You keep wanting to try for a baby and yet you are so stressed you are drinking scotch just to get through the day. This is not the environment I want our baby to be born into, Jay."

He exhales heavily, knowing I'm right.

The thing is, I've already been secretly trying for a baby. As soon as he told me he wanted a baby, I went off the pill. I know I should have told him, but lovemaking is Jameson's safe place, the only time where he completely switches off and gets lost in the moment.

When he needs an escape from pressure, he has me, and we have this.

A beautiful act between two people in love.

And I know him, the minute I tell him that we are actively trying, he will tie it to a target and become obsessed and get stressed if we don't fall. I'd rather just surprise him when the time comes if we are blessed.

"I'm booking a vacation for us, we need to get away."

He rolls his eyes.

"And you are coming home with me now."

"I am *not* coming home now."

I lean over him and shut down his computer. "You have no say in it."

He sits still in his chair and I sit back down on his lap and take him into my arms. "Baby...listen to me. I love you; I want us to have a long and healthy life together. Don't you want that?"

"I do."

"It's time to unplug for a little while. Do you really think that I can't feel what's going on inside of you at the moment?"

His eyes hold mine.

"The deadlines and spreadsheets, the directors...all of it means nothing if you have no quality of life." I kiss him softly and brush the hair back from his forehead, "You have an extremely high-pressured job and it's only natural that you get wound up. But you need to learn how to switch off. You are not at your best when you are like this, not to me, or Miles Media, or your brothers and parents. Least of all to yourself."

His hands tighten around me as he listens.

"Wouldn't it be great to come into work each morning feeling refreshed and rested? To not have your mind racing between the million tabs that are open."

He exhales heavily, and I know that he knows that I'm right.

"We're going home." I pull him up by the hand and straighten the desk up. I collect his things and put his brief-case over my shoulder. I lead him out through reception and the girls look up when they see us.

"I'm leaving for the day," he tells Sammia.

"Yes, okay." She smiles. "Good idea."

"And he's taking some time off, I just have to work out with Tristan when he can come and cover for him," I add.

"We'll see about that." Jameson rolls his eyes. "I'm being hijacked, Sammia, do you see this?"

Sammia smiles and we walk into the elevator, the doors close and we turn to face them.

"You know what the girls on reception are talking about right now?" he says casually.

"That I love you and that I'm taking care of my husband's mental health?" I smile goofily up at him.

"No." He straightens his tie. "Not even close."

"Then what are they saying?"

"That you smell like come." He grabs my sex with his hand.

"Stop." I laugh out loud as I swat him away as I look up at the cameras. "I do not smell like come," I splutter.

Oh my god, do I?

He throws me a sexy wink. "Trust me, you do."

———

The car pulls into the large circular driveway as nerves dance in my stomach.

I did it.

I got Jameson to take time off and come away; Tristan is covering at work for him and everything is going exactly to plan.

There's just one little problem.

Jay thinks we are in Thailand to go to a fancy resort, I haven't told him we are actually here to go to a wellness retreat.

No alcohol, healthy food, meditation, daily Chinese medicine healing sessions, tai chi, Pilates, and massages.

Jameson Miles' worst nightmare.

He frowns as he looks out of the car window. "What is this?"

"Surprise." I smile hopefully.

He raises an eyebrow. "What do you mean, surprise?"

"Well." I lean over him and open his door. "We wanted to wind down and this is the place to do it."

"What do you mean?"

Damn it, I'm going to have to just come out with it.

"We are booked into a wellness retreat, baby. Isn't this great?"

"What?" He pulls the car door closed. "No way in fucking hell, Emily."

"Jameson," I say sternly. "Get out of the car."

"No." He pushes the lock down on the door. "This is the relaxing holiday you booked," he whispers angrily. "I can't fucking believe you."

The driver chuckles from the front seat.

"This is not funny," Jameson snaps. "Drive."

The driver's eyes flick to mine in the rearview mirror for approval.

"Do not drive," I snap. "Stop being a big baby. Get out of the car, Jameson. Right now."

"Absolutely not." He crosses his arms. "I am *not* staying in this godforsaken fucking hippy place."

"Well, I am."

"Good. Have fun eating grass."

Seriously?

"Jameson, I want to wind down and this is where I want to do it. Can't you just come here for me?"

"No."

I begin to get angry.

"It's either this or camping for a month in Thailand, the choice is yours," I snap. "And it's wet season and the mosquitos are Jurassic Park sized."

He opens his mouth to say something and I cut him off.

"I'm not even joking, Jameson. Do not piss me off," I whisper angrily. "I am sick to death of living with a fucking stress head so if you can't come here and try to relax for me, then why are we even married? What is the fucking point?"

He narrows his eyes and glares at me.

I get out of the car in a huff, I *am* going in and if he doesn't stay here with me it's going to be World War Three.

Prepare yourself, fucker.

The driver pops the trunk and gets out to help me with the bags. "Just the one?" he asks.

"Both bags," I snap.

If he isn't staying then he's not getting his things either, screw him.

Thankfully I'm smarter than him.

I knew he would do this so in a premeditated attack I snuck the credit cards out of his wallet while we were on the plane. He has to stay, whether he likes it or not.

Even if he leaves now, he has to come back later.

I begin to roll the two large suitcases down the driveway and I can feel him watching me from the car.

Is he coming?

I get to the grand front steps and two doormen run out to meet me. "Hello, hello." They smile as they grab my suitcases from me. "Let me take those."

"Thank you." I smile as I glance back at the car and see Jameson's scowling face through the car window.

I can't fucking believe him.

I walk to the front reception desk. "Hello, welcome. Can I help you?" The receptionist smiles.

"Yes." I smile awkwardly as I slide over my credit card. "I'm checking in today. The name is Emily Miles."

I glance over my shoulder to see the car I arrived in has gone.

He left?

I begin to hear my angry heartbeat in my ears, I went to so much trouble and begged them to fit us in because they were booked out and then I had to keep it a secret and the whole rigmarole and he fucking left without even looking at the place. Typical pigheaded Jameson Miles.

This means war.

The kind receptionist types into her computer as I wait in silence.

Where's he going to go? He has no money. Then I remember who he is.

Who am I kidding? He could talk his way into any five-star resort, they probably have a poster of his face in their staff rooms.

Boom, boom, boom...my angry heartbeat sounds in my ears.

"I have you in the deluxe penthouse for the entirety of your stay."

I force a smile. "Thank you, that sounds wonderful."

"You'll be shown to your room and then your master will come and collect you and give you the tour."

I frown, confused. "Okay?"

"Master?" Jameson says flatly from behind me. "Master of what?"

I jump, startled by his voice, and turn back toward him and relief fills me.

You're so lucky.

"Don't talk to me," he mouths, he steps to the desk in front of me as he attempts to take over. "How long is the booking for?"

"Twenty-one days."

"Twenty-one...." He rolls his fingers on the desk as he gives me the side eye. "Yeah, that's not happening. We will be checking out tomorrow, thank you."

She smiles up at him and then at me as if hearing this conversation many times before.

"Bjorn. Can you show Mr. and Mrs. Miles to their suite, please?"

"Sure." A big burly blond man wearing all white comes over. "This way, please." He takes off in front of us and I go to grab Jameson's hand and he flicks me away. "Don't touch me."

"Your room is through the garden of tranquility," Bjorn says in a monotone voice. "We must give thanks as we walk through and into the next stage of your life."

Jameson rolls his eyes. "Fuck me," he mouths.

I bite my lip to hide my smile.

We follow him out through the double doors and through the most beautiful garden, I have to admit, it really is very tranquil.

Perfectly manicured lush green lawns and perfect gardens. There's a huge water feature in the middle with a waterfall coming out of it down to a lower-level garden where lilies are floating. Bjorn stops in front of it, closes his eyes and bows with his hands in a praying gesture.

Jameson grabs his dick and I put my face into my hands.

Oh my god.

"Come, join me, give thanks," Bjorn says.

"Okay." I put my hands in a praying gesture like his and try to copy what he's doing.

Jeez, this really is over the top.

Maybe Jameson is right and this is going to be one giant clusterfuck.

"Where is my room?" Jameson snaps impatiently from behind us.

Bjorn looks Jameson square in the eye and smiles calmly, so calmly that it's kind of eerie. "This way." He walks in front of us.

Jameson taps his temple. "He's fucking tapped," he mouths. "Probably a serial killer."

I'm beginning to wonder.

We follow him through gardens and down winding paths and over a bridge and my god, this property really is magical.

We finally get to a beautiful cabana overlooking the sea. "This is your new home for the foreseeable future."

"Wow," I gush, I turn to see that even Jameson is a little impressed.

Bjorn opens the front door and we are hit in the face with a stark simplicity. All white furnishings, walls, ceilings and floors.

We walk in and look around. "It's...beautiful." I smile. "Wow."

Bjorn points to two large baskets. "First thing you need to do is to wash off the world."

"Wash off the what?" Jameson frowns.

"Shower using the salt scrub in the pots, rub it into your skin as a cleanse. Wash each other, enjoy the experience."

Jameson's stone-cold eyes stare at Bjorn.

"Put all of your possessions into these baskets." He taps

the basket and then hands us white outfits that look similar to scrubs. "These are the clothes that you will adorn while here. There are no personal possessions to distract you."

Jameson stares at him as if his brain is misfiring.

"This will free you, Mr. Miles."

"Or free you to steal my shit."

"Put all electronics and your clothes into the baskets and leave your suitcases by the door. We will put those into storage, you may keep your toiletries bag if you wish, but we would prefer you to use our organic products for your stay."

"No phones?" I frown.

"No internet, and no phones," Bjorn replies. "No watches, no time. No distractions."

"Oh, for fuck's sake." Jameson sighs. "I'm out."

Bjorn smiles calmly. "Shower, wash the world off each other and then your master will come to collect you."

"To do what?" Jameson snaps.

"Tonight you both have a two-hour massage followed by a hot oil bath, a beautiful dinner followed by an offering of tropical fruit."

Jameson puts his weight onto his back foot and I can tell even he likes the sound of that.

I smile goofily. "Thank you, that sounds wonderful."

He bows his head and without another word he walks out the door and closes it behind him.

"What the hell were you thinking?" Jameson snaps.

I shrug. "It's fun."

"Nothing about this is fucking fun, Emily."

"We get to wash the world off each other." I try to sweeten the deal.

"I have never been less aroused than I am in this moment."

I put my hand over my mouth and laugh. "Just get in the shower."

"You get in the fucking shower," he whispers angrily. "I am not putting my phone in that stupid fucking basket."

"Three days."

"What?"

"If you do what they ask for three days, we can leave." I hold the towel out to him.

"Newsflash deluded one. I'll leave whenever I fucking want."

I put my hands onto my hips. "Get in the shower before I drown you in it."

He drags his hand down his face and once again I get the giggles. "You have to admit this is pretty funny."

"Not one bit." He snatches the towel from me. "You don't need to drown me, I'm drowning myself." He storms into the bathroom and closes the door behind him.

I open the door and peer around it. "I thought we were washing each other."

"Get out before you cause a murder-suicide," he growls, infuriated.

I giggle again.

He showers and walks out with a towel around his waist and sees that I've already put my things into the basket.

"You're really putting your phone in there?"

"Uh-huh,"

"What if there's an emergency?"

"Tristan will call us here."

"He knows about this?" he fumes.

"He found this place for me."

"I'm going to fucking kill him with my bare hands."

I go up onto my tippy-toes and kiss his big, beautiful lips.

"Please, Jay, if you can't do this for you. Do it for me." I put his hand over my stomach. "For our future."

He exhales deeply as his eyes hold mine.

"Three days is all I'm asking."

He hesitates and I know he wants to leave, but I also know that deep down he would do anything to make me happy. "Fine."

I bounce on the spot. "Thank you." I pass him the white outfit and he begrudgingly puts it on. The linen pants are white and baggy with a matching shirt.

"Oh, you look like a hot dentist." I smile excitedly.

"It's ironic that you say that." He looks down at himself, unimpressed. "I'm currently imagining pulling your teeth out, one by one."

I giggle, I really wish I could record his reactions to things so I could watch it back later, this is comedy gold.

I shower and dress in the white scrubs and walk out to find Jameson sitting on the bed. "Did you put your phone into the basket?" I ask.

"Yes."

"And your watch?"

He raises his eyebrow.

I smile. "Good boy."

He closes his eyes as if searching for divine guidance. "Don't patronize me, Emily, I'm on the fucking edge."

Knock, knock sounds at the door.

"You better get that; Master Splinter is here," he mutters dryly.

I open the door to see an older Thai man, he's wearing a deep red cloak and looks all mystical like a Tibetan monk or something. "Hello."

He gives me a calm smile. "Hello, my child."

My heart skips a beat. *Oh he feels magical.*

"My name is Chakrii; I am your master for your stay here."

"Hello, I'm Emily and this is my husband, Jameson." I introduce us.

Jameson stands and shakes his hand. "Hello."

Chakrii smiles and holds Jameson's hand in his, he frowns up at him. "Your mind is very busy."

Hit the nail on the head.

Jameson glares at him.

"Yes," I reply. "That's why we're here. He needs to find his peace."

Chakrii smiles. "You've come to the right place, my friend."

Jameson stays silent and I know that he must be able to feel Chakrii's presence like I can.

"Come, let's do the tour."

Over the next hour we walk all over the most beautiful resort I have ever seen; we see temples and healing rooms, gardens, and gymnasiums, we walk through the kitchens and meet the chefs. Wander through the waterfalls and over the streams.

Wow, I am awed by this place.

We end up on a cliff face overlooking the ocean, the sun is just setting over the water and Chakrii sits cross-legged on a huge rock shelf and looks out over the sea.

"Sit." He taps the rock beside him. "Be at one with nature."

I sit down on the rock and Jameson exhales heavily. "How much are we paying to sit on this fucking rock?" he mutters under his breath.

I widen my eyes at him and with a subtle shake of his head he eventually sits down beside me.

"Close your eyes," Chakrii tells us. "Inhale the sea air." He inhales deeply through his nose, and then exhales through his mouth. "Breathe in the sea air and breathe out to release your worries. Imagine the problems of the world leaving your body as if they are a tangible force." He continues to breathe in and out with his eyes closed. "A flower...coming back to life. Feel yourself be reborn unto this earth."

Jameson's face is flat and uninterested and I really want to laugh out loud, but I won't. I tap him on the leg. "Close your eyes," I mouth.

"Fuck off," he mouths back.

I close my eyes and try to follow Chakrii's breathing pattern and after a while I open one eye to see what Jameson is doing.

He's staring at me deadpan.

"What are you doing?" I whisper.

"Judging you."

I get the giggles and close my eyes.

We sit on the rock for a long time, the sun slowly sets over the water and it gets darker.

"Are we done here?" Jameson asks.

"We will never be done here." Chakrii smiles as if he knows a secret, he continues to breathe deeply in through his nose and out through his mouth.

"Well, I'm done here." Jameson stands. "My ass is hurting. I'll see you back at the room." He storms off, my heart sinks as I watch him disappear over the hill.

Chakrii smiles calmly and takes my hand in his. "It takes time, my child, do not worry about your husband. Concentrate on your own journey."

He holds my hand in his and we sit on the rock and stare out to sea.

I feel a little deflated, a little pensive, and I'm wondering if I have done the right thing, I really hope this works out.

Two wonderful hours of the best massage I've ever had, a hot oil bath and now this.

We are sitting at a private dining table on the beach, candles are on the table and the waiters are serving up our dinner. The sound of the waves gently lapping at the shore are echoing up the mountain.

My god, this place is heaven.

Jameson is quiet but even he can't deny how amazing today has been.

The last of our food is set out on the table and Jameson eyes it suspiciously. "Where is the meat?" he asks.

"We are vegan."

Jameson's face falls. "Vegan?"

"I trust you will enjoy your meal, sir." The waiter smiles. "Try it, you will be pleasantly surprised. Our chefs are world class."

"Any chance of a glass of wine?" Jameson asks.

"No, sir."

"Not even the organic vegan shitty type?"

"No, sir."

"That's fine, thank you." I cut them off.

The waiter leaves us alone and Jameson exhales. "You know, when I met you on the plane and you guessed that I was married to a vegan yoga nut, you failed to mention that you planned on turning into her." He sits back in his chair. "Was this your strategic plan all along?"

I smile softly and take his hand over the table. "I love you." I lift his hand and kiss the back of it. "So much."

He gives me a stifled smile. "You better."

My heart swells, he doesn't hate me after all.

"Yoga starts tomorrow," I reply.

"Oh goody, I can't wait," he mutters dryly.

We eat our dinner and just as promised, it's beautiful. The fresh fruit for dessert is divine.

"I'm so sleepy from my massage," I say with a stretch. "How do you feel?"

"Slimy."

"What?" I frown.

"That oil bath is up in my regions; I've got slimy ass cheeks, I'm about to slip off this chair."

I burst out laughing and so does he.

Tomorrow is a new day.

———

I wake with a start, alone in bed.

The light filtering through the windows tells me it's early, but where is Jameson?

I climb out of bed and walk out of the bedroom to see him on the front veranda.

I watch him for a moment, wearing his all whites, he walks up and then he walks back. He walks up and then back.

Pacing, like a caged animal.

"Good morning," I say as I walk out through the door.

"Hi." His hands are on his hips and he's completely distracted.

"What's wrong?"

"They took my things; I don't have my runners."

"Oh." I drop to sit on the steps. "You missed your run?"

He walks up and then he walks back.

"What time do you reckon it is?" he asks.

"Does it matter?"

"Yes, it fucking matters. I don't have time to just hang around here all fucking day and do nothing."

"There's lots of fucking in that sentence."

"Don't start."

Jeez.

He walks up and then he walks back, he walks up and then he walks back.

What the hell? Why is he so wound up?

"Good morning," a voice calls, we look up to see a big burly man in the white uniform. "I'm Jarden, I'm here for your stretch class." He has a yoga mat under his arm.

Jameson narrows his eyes. "The what?"

"We start our day with breath work and stretching."

"For the love of god." Jameson sighs. "Make it stop."

I roll my lips to hide my smile. "He can go first." I stand, I have to let them take over, Jameson is obviously having some kind of episode here. I walk back inside and peer through the curtains to secretly watch.

Jarden rolls out the mat onto the sand. "Lie down on your stomach."

"What do you mean?"

"On your stomach."

Jameson lies down on his stomach and Jarden begins to rub his back, he puts his hands in his hair and begins to massage his scalp, Jameson swats his hand away. "My scalp doesn't need stretching, you fool."

I put my hand over my mouth to stop myself from

laughing out loud.

Honestly.

He steps over Jameson so that he has one foot either side of his body and grabs his two arms and pulls them. "Ahh," Jameson complains.

Jarden puts his foot between Jameson's shoulder blades and really begins to pull his arms back.

"The fuck are you doing?" Jameson cries. "Arms don't bend that way, I'm not a contortionist."

I watch on as they go through the moves and then Jarden instructs him to roll over onto his back. He picks up Jameson's feet and brings them up over his shoulders until his toes touch the ground.

"Ahhh," Jameson cries. "Are you trying to break me in fucking half?"

I do burst out laughing this time, I wish I had my phone so I could take a photo.

As they go through the moves, Jameson fights Jarden at every turn.

Until eventually it becomes too painful to watch, I'm taking a shower.

Jameson

Day three in hell.

I pace back and forth, unable to sit still. I've had healing sessions, I've had acupuncture, massages every day. Attempted yoga, had the shit stretched out of me every morning at the crack of dawn, I've had meditation...well, I judged the idiots who meditated. Not a drop of alcohol and

I have a splitting fucking headache from caffeine and protein withdrawal.

You name it, I've done it.

And how do I feel?

Anxious, irritable, perspiring like a pig, and fuck this.

I'm a million times more wound up here than I ever have been at home.

I just need to leave.

"Jay, you've got another healing session," Emily reminds me.

"I'm not going." I shake my head, defeated. "I can't do this, Em."

"I know this is hard."

"I just...I need to leave, babe. I've never felt so unhinged."

Her eyes search mine as she cups my face in her hand. "I'm really enjoying it."

"You stay." I pull her into a hug. "I just can't.... I'm leaving. I'll wait for you in another hotel."

"You're detoxing." A voice sounds from behind us.

We turn to see Master Chakrii.

"Your mind doesn't know what to do," he says calmly.

I frown.

"Coming off adrenaline is like coming off heroin. You are effectively a drug addict whose body is addicted to stress. As your mind declutters, your body goes into a panic, unsure of what to do."

My jaw clenches as I stare at the master.

"You're nearly through the worst of it, don't give up now, you've come so far."

"This isn't working," I reply softly.

I've never felt so defeated.

"It is, I promise you. Your body is purging pent-up stress. If you leave before you have gone through the process you will be right back where you left off."

"How long do you think it will it take?" Emily asks.

"Another week."

"A week?" I gasp. "I'll be dead in another week here."

Chakrii puts his hand on my shoulder. "Trust me, my friend. Trust the process. You need to stop fighting against it."

Unexpected emotion fills my every cell and I get a lump in my throat; I know I need to get a handle on the way I live.

Emily deserves more than having a workaholic stressed-out husband, and I would give anything to be that for her...but this...my eyes flick between the two of them.

"Jay," Emily says softly as she takes my hands in hers. "You can do this, baby, I know you can. We can do it together."

I close my eyes; the truth is, I really don't think I can.

I'm letting her down.

"I don't know how to stop my mind," I whisper.

"Then you learn," Chakrii says. "You take it minute by minute, hour by hour."

I stare at him as I listen.

"And then one day, something will let go."

My sanity?

"Like what?" I ask.

"The pressure of expectation," Chakrii replies.

I frown, it's like he's reading my mind.

"You are not the first corporate highflier we have had here; you will not be the last. The ones that leave early...." His voice trails off.

"What?" Emily asks. "What happens to the ones that leave early?"

"Some return, sometimes years later when they realize the truth."

"What truth?" Emily asks.

"That there is no easy way, you have to push through the barriers that your thoughts have created for you." He smiles wistfully. "To be able to control your mind is the greatest strength that one can have."

Isn't that the truth.

"So you need to make a decision, Jameson, right now. Are you going to go through life wondering what could have been?"

Emily takes my hand in hers and kisses my fingertips.

"Or are you going to tough it out and stay?" He pauses as if choosing his words wisely. "Twenty-one days could change the whole trajectory of your life, do you want to feel free?"

I feel like the weight of the world is on my shoulders... because it is. It feels like it always has been. My life is a gift, one that I want more than anything.

Without a word, I walk inside and go into the bathroom and stare at my reflection in the mirror. I take a long hard look at myself and my eyes well with tears because I don't like what I see.

I know I have to do this.

Emily walks into the bathroom and puts her arms around me from behind and kisses my shoulder. She doesn't say anything, she just holds me while I have my meltdown.

A knock sounds at the door. "Jameson," a voice calls.

"Yes?"

"It's Jarden, I'm here for your stretch class."

What's it going to be, sink or swim?

Swim.

"I'll be right out."

Emily

I sit on the front porch of our bungalow and read through the notes in my diary, I've been keeping a score of what goes down in here and I have to say, it's been very satisfying to go back and read through it day by day.

We are making progress, and on the days where I felt we have gone backward, I've returned to the diary to recap and remind myself of where we were at the beginning.

Day one, a total disaster.

Day two, Jameson paced for hours. I think he's losing his mind.

Day three, Jameson had a meltdown and thankfully decided to stay.

Day seven, Jameson actually closed his eyes during meditation. I think we could be onto something here.

Day eight, he had a major meltdown, he wanted to leave and find a restaurant because he needed to eat a steak.

Day ten, he stopped pacing and for the first time since I've known Jay, he is calm and present.

Day thirteen and fourteen, he slept for two days straight, Master Chakrii says this is a breakthrough and that his body is releasing the last of his stored adrenaline. To be honest it's kind of scary for me to see him like this, Jameson never sleeps so for him to do it for two full days and nights is unsettling.

Day fifteen, we laughed all day and then made love under the stars on the beach.

Day by day and little by little, I can feel Jameson purging old beliefs, breaking destructive habits. Reacting to the Chinese medicine and discovering a new sense of self.

I begin to write my next entry.

Day eighteen.

I glance up from my diary to see my man sitting up on the cliff on the rock ledge, staring out to sea.

Cross-legged and pensive, he's been up there for hours, alone and just being in the moment with nature.

He's not complaining or whining or being a sarcastic asshole to anyone.

I smile softly, I've never loved him more.

Day twenty-one.

My back arching off the bed wakes me from a deep sleep and instantly I know where I am.

In bed, on my back with my legs over my Jameson's shoulders, his fingers spreading me wide, his tongue licking me deep, he's sucking and nibbling and my back arches again, oh fuck, I'm about to come.

How long has he been doing this?

I moan as my fingers twist in his hair. "Oh god," I whimper as I spread my legs wider.

He smiles into me. "Good morning, Mrs. Miles."

"It sure is."

Seriously, *how is this my life?*

He licks me deeper and I begin to shudder. "Stop," he commands as he slides up my body, bringing my legs over his shoulders.

We fall silent as we stare at each other, the air buzzing with deep arousal.

When he has me in this position I am completely at his mercy, my body is his for the taking. To fuck and use however he wants.

He knows it and he loves it.

And so do I.

His eyes are dark and dangerous and I feel the tip of his thick cock slide through my swollen lips. He finds the sweet spot and pushes in hard, my body fluttering around his as it tries to deal with his size.

His eyes roll back in his head and then he slowly slides out and then pushes in hard, the bed hits the wall as he lets me have it with both barrels.

Deep punishing hits, his thick cock taking exactly what it needs from my body.

And in return, mine accepting all of his. Sucking him in as if my life depends on it, because at this moment, it does.

He is all that I need.

Everything seems magnified in here, the laughter, the love that we make, the time in each other's arms. Perhaps it's because there are no distractions, or maybe because we've crossed another emotional bridge. I don't know what it is, but everything feels like more. The highest of highs, I'm grateful, so grateful.

I cry out as an orgasm tears through me and then he slams in and holds himself deep.

I feel the telling jerk of his cock as it empties deep inside of me and we pant as we try to catch our breath.

He smiles down at me. "Let's go home."

Jameson

"Renata, where are we on the Robinson deal?" I ask.

"I'm waiting for them to get back to me with the contract," she replies across the board table.

"Why are you waiting? Chase it up."

"Yes sir." She scribbles in her diary and a knock sounds at the door.

"Yes," I call.

Sammia sticks her head around the door. "Jameson, can I see you for a moment, please?"

"I'm in a meeting, Sammia, you can see that."

"It's urgent, sir."

Fuck's sake. "Excuse me." I stand and walk out of the room. "What is it?"

"You have a visitor in your office."

"Who?"

"Emily, she says that it's extremely urgent."

What's wrong?

I march to my office and barge open the door, Emily is sitting at my desk. "What's wrong?" I splutter.

She bounces out of the chair and kisses me softly as she wraps her arms around me. "Nothing, everything is right."

I peel her arms off from around me. "I am in a board meeting, Emily," I whisper. "What are you doing?"

"I just thought you'd like to know the news."

"Know what?"

She digs around in her bag and pulls something out and passes it over to me.

"What's this?"

"A pregnancy test. One line for negative, two lines for positive."

Two lines.

I frown as I stare at it in my hands.

My eyes rise to meet hers. "But we didn't start trying yet."

She smiles softly. "Maybe we did."

With my heart in my throat, I stare at my beautiful wife.

What?

"You're going to be a daddy, Jay." She smiles up at me.

What?

"Are you sure?"

She shrugs and then laughs. "I did two tests."

I take her into my arms and hold her tight, so tight I nearly break her.

"You're squashing me." She laughs against my shoulder. "Ouch."

"Oh my god." I put my hand on her stomach. "Are you okay?"

"I don't know." She shrugs. "I've never done this before, I think so."

I take her face into my hands and I kiss her. *This woman.*

This beautiful woman, she came into my life and loved me and saved me from myself.

And now this....

Emotion overwhelms me and I get a lump in my throat as I stare down at her.

I can't believe it, there are no words to describe what I'm feeling.

So much love.

"Are you still going to love me when I get fat?" She smiles up at me.

I chuckle and take her into my arms and walk her backward toward my desk. "Try and stop me."

Emily

A text bounces into my phone:

I'm here

I go to the window and look down to the street and see Scott standing to the side of the front doors of the building, the blacked-out SUV Audi parked in the loading zone.

My escort home is here.

True to Jameson Miles' overprotective style I have been wrapped in cotton wool.

In my first trimester I suffered greatly from morning sickness and one day when I was looking especially green, a photographer was hassling me and I slipped on the pavement and nearly fell over.

Jameson went ballistic, and since that day I have had a personal bodyguard with me whenever we are in New York, which is Monday to Friday.

I hated it at first, and we fought about it often. But now as I'm at the end of my second trimester, I do have to admit I feel safer. Not from murdering killers or anything dramatic like that, the paparazzi are the only ones I need protecting from.

I walk back to my desk and close down my computer and look around my office.

I only have six weeks left at work and I'm a little sad, I'm going to miss my office, I really love my job and the independence it's given me.

But we've decided that we are moving to our house in the country, Arndell, full time once the baby is born, Jameson will work from home two days a week and commute the other three.

We really want the baby to grow up barefoot, climbing trees and playing in the mud.

Hidden away in our own little cocoon of love.

We've had some renovations done on the house in preparation for being there full-time, new bathrooms and kitchen, new carpet, and furnishings. Every time we go there we take a little bit more of our personal belongings. The plan is to have both the country house and the penthouse in New York fully equipped so that we can just move between the two without the need to pack bags.

We're so excited to get there, once the baby is born Jameson has three weeks off for us to settle in as a family.

I can't wait.

We would move beforehand but my doctor and the hospital are in New York and Jameson couldn't handle the stress of being two hours away if I go into early labor.

My phone beeps another text.

Are you okay?

Jeez, I text back.

Coming now.

I grab my bag and make my way downstairs; Scott is

standing by the double glass doors as he waits for me. "Good afternoon, Emily."

"Hi, Scott." I smile as he walks me to the car. "How was your day?" I ask him.

"Great, and yours?" He opens the car door and I glance in to see Jameson sitting in the back seat, navy suit, square jaw and the best come fuck-me-look of all time.

"It just got a lot better." I smile as I climb in.

"Mrs. Miles." Jameson smiles, he takes my face in his hands and kisses me softly.

"This is a nice surprise."

"I thought I'd take you out to dinner." He kisses me again. "Then you can eat me for dessert."

I laugh out loud. "You're a bona fide sex maniac."

He takes my hand in his and gives me a playful wink.

I'm not even joking, I thought once my pregnancy body set in he would calm down.

He is more obsessed with me now than ever.

We arrive at the restaurant and Scott pulls the car over and gets out and opens the car door, Jameson climbs out first and then helps me out.

"There he is," we hear as cameras click.

Jameson puts his head down and with my hand in a vise-like grip we walk through the circus of paparazzi.

"Back off," I hear Scott demand from behind us. "Move out of the way."

We walk into the restaurant and instantly return to earth. It's calm and serene and piano music is playing in the background. It's like another world in here, away from the crazy.

"Good evening, Mr. and Mrs. Miles." The waiter smiles. "I have your favorite table waiting, sir."

"Thank you," Jameson replies, as we walk through to our

table, I see people turning their heads to look our way and I drop my head and smile at the floor, I should be used to it by now, but I'm not, I don't think I ever will be.

Nothing has changed in New York.

Jameson Miles attracts attention wherever he goes.

He always will.

———

I wake to the feeling of period pain and I frown and glance at the clock on my bedside table: 2.55 a.m.

What's happening?

Another pang of ache rolls through me and I wince.

Oww.... Okay, that's...uncomfortable.

I glance over to Jay as he sleeps beside me and I quietly get up and walk downstairs and go to the bathroom. I have this heavy feeling in my stomach and down below, but I'm not due for another ten days.

It must be Braxton-Hicks. Please don't be in labor, I have shit I need to get done before you arrive, bubba.

I rub my big tummy, it's a weird feeling, not a pain, more of an ache and now I have heartburn, fuck's sake.

I feel like shit.

Maybe it was the Indian food we had for dinner.

I sit on the toilet for a while, I feel hot and clammy and ugh, don't tell me I have a tummy bug.

I eventually get into the shower and lean up against the wall, the hot water feels nice on my skin. I close my eyes; I wish I could sleep standing, I'm so, so, tired.

"Emily?" I hear Jameson's panicked voice as he comes flying into the bathroom, his eyes are wide. "What's happening?"

"I'm fine, heartburn." I wondered how long it would be until he woke up and came looking for me.

He looks down at the floor of the shower. "It doesn't look like heartburn."

Huh?

I glance down to see that the water running down the drain is a pretty shade of pink.

"Oh crap."

"What do you mean oh crap?"

"My waters have broken."

"Oh...fucking hell.... Crap," he cries. "It's too early."

"It's fine, we're ready."

"I'm glad you are," he snaps, all flustered. "I am not fucking ready." He runs from the bathroom and I roll my eyes, of course he is going to be all Jameson Miles dramatic-like.

The hot water feels so nice on my skin and I close my eyes as I continue to lean against the wall.

"Yes." I hear Jameson's voice and he walks into the bathroom on his phone. "She's in the shower." He listens again. "Okay." He puts the phone down. "How long has this been going on?"

"What do you mean?"

He holds his hand out to the floor. "That," he stammers.

"Well, you just discovered it, so not long."

"Fucking hell," he mutters to himself. "Not long." He listens again. "Are you having contractions?" he asks me.

"Just an ache."

"Just an ache." He frowns and begins to pace. "Alright then." He listens again. "Well it's hard to tell, she's pretty tough. Not much fazes her."

His eyes flick up to me and I smile, if only he could see

himself, stark naked and pacing in the bathroom while on the phone.

"Okay, see you soon." He hangs up. "We need to go to the hospital."

"Alright." I close my eyes as I lean up against the wall.

"Don't go to sleep. Emily. Now."

"Alright," I snap, half annoyed. "I'm fine, Jameson."

"I am *not*." He steps into the shower and turns it off. "Get out. Get out right this minute."

"Fuck's sake."

"Do not *fuck's sake* me," he splutters as he holds a towel up for me. "We need to go and we need to go now. This is an emergency."

"Aren't you supposed to be the one keeping me calm?" I snap as I take the towel from him.

His face falls as he realizes what he's doing. "Yes, yes I am. True." He exhales deeply as he remembers what to do. "This is fine, it's all fine and you don't need to worry because it's totally fine," he blurts out in a rush as he begins to pace again. "It's all going to be fine, Em. Perfectly fine."

I giggle. *Idiot.*

"So what you're saying is that it's all fine?" I tease.

He closes his eyes as he fights the urge to give me a sarcastic reply.

"That's right, sweetheart." He smiles as he tries his best to act cool. "We're going to get in the car and we're going to take a little trip to the hospital so that we can meet our baby," he says in the sweetest fakest voice I've ever heard.

I roll my eyes. "Don't think you are talking to me in that voice through labor, I'm going to vomit in my own mouth."

"What voice?"

"That sweet pathetic voice. Just be normal and say whatever it is that you want to say."

"Okay, fine." He exhales as if relieved. "Get in the fucking car, Emily, because I'm freaking the fuck out."

I burst out laughing.

"Is that better?" He smirks.

"Much better." I kiss his lips and he wraps his arms around me. "Can you believe this is happening?"

"Not really." He puts his two hands over my stomach and looks down at them. "This baby is going to be just like you." He smiles against my lips. "I can feel it."

"Today." Excitement fills me, "Oh my god, Jay, we get to meet our baby today."

He kisses me softly, his lips lingering over mine, and I wish we had all day to kiss, to take the time to enjoy the last hours of it being just us.

Our last alone time.

"We have to go," he tells me. "I'll grab the bag and you get dressed."

"Okay."

I walk into our bedroom and pull out a drawer, my stomach clenches hard and I stop on the spot. "Ouch...." The tightening hardens and hardens and keeps clenching until it really hurts, oh hell, this isn't...great.

"Is this a contraction?" My eyes widen in horror. "Don't tell me that's what it feels like."

"Tell you what?" Jameson replies as he walks into the room.

"I think I just had a contraction."

What did it feel like?"

"Pretty...." I pause as I search for the right word. "Hectic."

"Hectic?" He twists his lips. "All the more reason to hurry."

"Okay." I bend down to put my underpants on and another one hits, this time it's stronger and it doubles me over in pain. "Oh...jeez."

"What's happening?" His eyes widen. "What the fuck is happening right now?"

"A contraction."

"Another one?"

I nod.

"What do you mean, that's too close together."

My breathing becomes labored as I try to deal with it.

Fuck, this is full on.

"Get in the fucking car. Get in the fucking car. Right now!" He bends and holds my underpants open so that I can step into them, he pulls them up at speed and then pulls my dress on over my head.

"I need a bra."

"Why? Trust me, nobody is going to be looking at your tits."

I get the giggles.

"Do not start with your giggling now, woman."

I put my shoes on and he grabs my hospital bag and we head out the door, the biggest thing that Jameson has wanted through my pregnancy is to drive me to the hospital himself. For some reason, it's really important to him. I just hope this all goes to plan.

We get to the elevator and my stomach hardens again; I stop and screw my face up.

Shit.

"Breathe," he says.

I pant. "Did you learn how to say that in prenatal classes?"

"Yes. I did actually, smart-ass."

I smile up at him.

"Even in labor." He rolls his eyes. "Un-fucking-believable."

We get in the elevator and ride to the basement parking lot, he takes my hand in his and marches us across to the car, another contraction hits and it knocks the wind out of me. "Ahh," I moan as I stop on the spot, my breathing is labored and I'm beginning to perspire.

"Babe, you're scaring me. Should I call an ambulance?" He waits patiently as I have my moment. "This seems to be progressing very fast."

"No, it's fine. Let's go."

"Maybe I should take a look," he says as we get to the car, he opens the door for me.

"At what?" I frown as I climb in.

"To see if I can see the head."

"You fucking idiot, you will not be able to see the head," I snap, infuriated. Another contraction hits and it's the hardest yet, shattering pain sears through me. "Ahhh." I cry as I grip the dashboard.

Jameson's eyes widen and he takes off with speed, he floors it out of the parking lot so fast that the car flies through the air. "Cross your legs," he snaps, his eyes are darting between me and the road.

"I have a watermelon trying to smash its way out, crossing my legs is not going to fucking stop it."

"Jesus." Jameson is perspiring as we fly through the streets of New York.

I get another contraction and I cry out in pain. "Ahhh."

"Ahhhhhh," he cries too as he reaches over and tries to put his hand up my dress. "What are you doing?" I yell.

"Just putting my hand there to stop it coming out."

I swat him away. "You are the dumbest smart man I

know," I cry.

A few contractions and in the quickest time known to man we make it to the hospital and Jameson parks out the front in the no-standing area.

"You can't park here," I pant.

"I dare someone to try and stop me." He runs around and opens the door and helps me out. We make our way up to the maternity ward, and although we have been here before on our tour, it all seems so much more real now. Jameson makes his way to the nursing station. "Hello, I called before. Emily has gone into labor."

"Mr. Miles, yes." The nurse smiles. "This way."

We get to the room and the kind nurse hooks me up to a monitor and makes me comfortable. She seems so relaxed, just the opposite to how I'm currently feeling.

I wanted so badly to feel in control and calm, I was sure I was going to be a pro at this labor thing, so far I feel like a feral animal who is about to go through an exorcism.

The nurse smiles. "I'll leave you alone for a little while, I'll be back in a moment to check your reading."

"Thanks."

Bleep.

Bleep.

Bleep.

Bleep.

Jameson smiles as he stares at the baby's heartbeat monitor, "Look how strong that heartbeat is, Em." He sits on the side of the bed and smiles down at me; his demeanor has changed and he pushes the hair back from my forehead. "It's going to be fine."

Butterflies swirl in my stomach. "How do you know?"

"Because this baby has you as a mom."

My eyes well with tears.

"And its father loves its mother so, so much." He kisses my forehead.

Another contraction racks through my body and I begin to cry as fear fills me. "Jay, I don't think I can do this," I whisper in a panic. "I changed my mind; I changed my mind now."

He holds my hand through it, finally it ends and I slump back into the mattress.

"It's okay, sweetheart."

"Is it?" I sob. "I knew it was going to be bad, I thought I had it in the bag but nothing can prepare you for this. It's worse than I thought, Jay. Much worse."

"You're the strongest person I know, Em."

"I don't feel very strong right now."

"You've got this babe; I know you do." He holds my face in his hands and kisses me softly. "Bring our baby to life."

My eyes search his.

"If I could do this for you, I would," he whispers. "You know that I would."

And that right there, those words put a fire in my belly.

He *would* do anything for me.

It's me, it's all me, I'm the only one who can do this for us. There is no shortcut.

I want to meet our baby.

I nod, filled with renewed determination.

"Let's do this."

Jameson

Five and a half hours later, with my heart in my throat, I watch on as Emily, the love of my life, moves heaven and

earth.

This is without a doubt the most incredible thing I have ever borne witness to.

How women do this every day blows my mind, there are no words to describe the awe I have for the female race in this moment.

"Last push, Emily."

The midwife smiles.

Em bears down and pushes hard and the baby slides out, the nurse picks it up and turns it over. "It's a boy."

"Waaaaaa!"

"A boy?" Emily laughs in relief.

The room blurs as I kiss my beautiful wife. "I'm so proud of you." I hold her tight. "I love you so much, you did it, sweetheart, you did it." I smile through tears. "Look at him."

"I love you too."

"Waaaaaa!" The baby screams harder. "Waaaaaa!"

I laugh as I wipe the tears that are running down my face.

Hands down the best day of my life.

They put the baby up onto her chest and we both stare at him in awe.

Chubby and covered in a white film, the cutest baby I ever saw.

So surreal.

"James." Emily smiles down at her son. "You look like a James."

"You sure you want two of us?" I smile.

"Positive."

I hug Emily, close my eyes, and say a little prayer.

Thank you.

Emily

Seven days and seven nights is a long time to go without sleep. The sound of ten trumpets sounds through our bedroom, and it's coming from the cradle at the end of our bed.

"Waaaaaa! Waaaaaa! Waaaaaa!"

It seems James has a penchant for screaming. It's his favorite thing, he does it all day, he does it all night.

"Fuck me," Jameson whispers. "What the hell is wrong with this baby?"

I smile up at the ceiling in the dark. "Just lie there quietly and he might go back to sleep."

"Waaaaaa! Waaaaaa! Waaaaaa!"

"He's not going back to sleep."

I close my eyes, I'm honestly so exhausted that I can't deal with this.

"What do I do?" Jameson whispers.

"He's not hungry, check his nappy and, I don't know, take him for a walk or something, I need to sleep, Jay. I have to get up and feed him in two hours, I'm delirious. I can't deal with one more night of this."

"You think I can?"

Jameson gets up and picks up the baby and looks down at him,

"Waaaaaa! Waaaaaa! Waaaaaa!"

"What is wrong with you?"

"Waaaaaa! Waaaaaa! Waaaaaa!"

"You are supposed to be chill like your mother, not psychopathic like me."

"Waaaaaa! Waaaaaa! Waaaaaa!"

I smile with my eyes closed as I listen to them.

"You don't need to cry like that, nobody is murdering you...yet."

I smile into my pillow.

"He said he wants scotch in his bottle."

"He did not say that."

"Oh that's right, it was me, I want to drink scotch from the fucking bottle."

I giggle.

"Waaaaaa! Waaaaaa! Waaaaaa!"

"You're killing me, kid." He changes his nappy and swaddles him. "Let's go scream in the living room so Mom can sleep."

"Waaaaaa! Waaaaaa! Waaaaaa!"

"You're going in time-out, you naughty baby. Quit it."

I smile as I begin to drift back to sleep.

"Waaaaaa! Waaaaaa! Waaaaaa!" James' screams get softer as Jay takes him out of the bedroom.

I wake with a start; my breasts are pumping as I get a letdown.

"Shit, what time is it?" I sit up and rush out into the living room in a panic, and then smile when I see it.

Jameson is flat on his back on the couch with his son swaddled tightly and sleeping on his chest.

Not the first week I imagined having with our baby, there's been tears and tantrums, breastfeeding issues and crying, so much crying, but it's been precious just the same.

Jameson said something tonight that struck home with me.

This is Jameson Miles' son, he has his nature, of course he's going to be difficult.

And somehow, that makes me love my baby all the more, suddenly I know it's all going to be okay.

If there's anyone that can handle a strong-willed Miles man.

It's me.

————

I sit at the kitchen counter and read my magazine.

The kids are playing in the back garden, James is five, Imogen is four, Alexander is two, and I'm pregnant again.

We're running a damn breeding program over here.

To be fair, the last two pregnancies have been surprises, happy surprises, but surprises just the same.

We live in the country full-time now; the kids are barefoot and fancy free.

Living the life that we always wanted for them.

Simple and full of love.

We will move back to New York full time once the kids are high school age.

The sound of the chopper comes over the mountain and the kids all squeal with excitement and run to the back fence to watch it land.

The chopper lands, the door opens and Jameson steps out. Square jaw, dark hair and the best fitted navy suit in all of the land. Still got it, and then some.

I smirk, my husband is hot.

The kids all rush him and run around his feet, he picks up Alexander and puts him on his hip as they walk back to the house.

Daddy's home.

THE TAKEOVER EPILOGUE

1

THE TAKEOVER EPILOGUE

Claire

Monday morning.

TRISTAN AND FLETCHER'S first day at Anderson Media and while I'm getting to the office with everybody else at 9 a.m. They left home at their usual 6:30 a.m.

What are they doing here so early?

I get into the elevator on the ground floor and ride it up, my mind is in overdrive.

While I'm more grateful than words could ever express to Tristan for taking Anderson Media on, it isn't going to make the transition any easier.

He runs a tight ship, a super yacht with all the bells and whistles and a high-powered engine room.

I've been floating along on a raft made of twigs and string.

Two very different business models with two very

different outcomes. I know we have to adapt; I know things have to change.

He's assured me that he is going to ensure a smooth transition and that there will be no casualties, which is one thing, I guess.

The staff don't know he's starting today, he thought it was best that he be the person to break it to them. But reading between the lines I think he doesn't want me to have to deal with anything stressful now that I'm pregnant.

His only goal now is to protect me and the boys, this company is for them and god help anyone who stands in his way.

The elevator doors open and I look around.

"Good morning, Ms. Anderson," Tristan's sexy voice purrs.

I look over to see him standing to the side looking like god's gift to women. Perfectly fitted navy suit, crisp white shirt, and gray tie. His dark hair is messed up to just-fucked perfection. He has his hands in his pockets and is leaning his behind on a desk.

"Good morning, Tristan."

He smirks and looks at his watch. "Eight fifty-two," he says to Fletcher who is standing beside him.

Fletcher scribbles something onto the pad he is holding.

Huh.

"What are you doing?" I ask.

Tristan smiles. "Go to your office, darling, and please remember that I love you."

I frown, and the elevator doors open again, a girl steps out and Tristan stands and shakes her hand. "Good morning, Tristan Miles."

The girl looks up in awe at the god. "Hello, Mr. Miles."

"What is your name?" he asks.

"Melanie Right."

"Good morning, Melanie, this is Fletcher Anderson," he introduces him.

Fletcher shakes her hand. "How do you do?"

Melanie smiles and then scurries to her desk; Tristan looks over to Fletcher and glances at his watch. "Melanie Right, eight fifty-six."

My eyes widen, he's making a note of what time everyone gets here.

What the fuck?

"I need coffee." I march to my office and close the door behind me. "*Fuck.*"

It's fine, it's fine....

My door busts open and Marley charges in. "Oh my fuck, what is going on out there?"

"What?" I screw up my face. "Do I even want to know?"

"Evan just got sprayed for being seven minutes late."

"Oh crap."

"And Marlene just got sent home because she was dressed inappropriately for the office."

My eyes widen. "What was she wearing?"

"A black bra underneath a see-through blouse."

I put my hands over my face.

"To be fair, she does dress like a total ho every day," Marley replies. "She makes me want to vomit in my own mouth most of the time."

The door opens, and Fletcher comes into view. "Marley, Tristan is looking for you."

"Oh crap." Marley screws up her face. "Help." She marches out the door and into the firing line. I peer out the corner of the blinds and spy on the office goings-on.

. . .

Over the next five hours I watch on as Tristan and Fletcher make their way around to everyone's desk, they chat and talk and have a way that can only be described as unapologetic.

They know what they want and they know how to get it.

Their people skills are so mastered and so perfected that they have everyone eating out of the palm of their hand.

I watch Fletcher, dressed in a three-thousand-dollar suit, exuding confidence as he chats and takes notes on everyone. He's laughing and asking questions and oozing a certain X factor that can only be described as Miles-like.

It's become abundantly clear to me that every day he spends working with Tristan, he becomes a little less Anderson and a little more Miles.

He's turning into the man he was always meant to be.

A confident, knowledgeable, and hardworking man, and I have never been prouder.

We have a meeting scheduled at 3 p.m. this afternoon for all staff, and I have no idea what to expect.

But I'm trying to trust the process.

Three p.m., and I sit in the front row of the auditorium with Marley.

Tristan has hired a hall for the staff meeting this afternoon, he wanted everyone in the same room.

This is new territory; we have never done anything like this before.

Tristan and Fletcher are sitting on the stage where a microphone and podium are set up as they wait for all of the staff to pile in.

Eventually Tristan stands and goes to the podium. "Good afternoon, everyone," he says in his sexy deep voice. "Thank you for coming." He gives a smile to the audience as everyone hangs on his every word.

I'm taken back to that conference he spoke at in Épernay and how much I despised him from my seat in the audience. Never in a million years did I imagine this life I live now would ever come to fruition.

"It's been great to meet all of you today." He turns back and gestures to Fletcher. "Fletcher and I wanted to have this meeting to explain the new adventure that Anderson Media is about to undertake."

The crowd falls silent.

"Firstly, you may all be asking what the fuck is Tristan Miles doing here?" He gives a playful wink and everyone chuckles. "With Claire Anderson's permission I'm going to be as straight with you as I possibly can."

He clicks a remote and a photograph of Wade and me comes up onto the large screen. We are young, early twenties, and sitting at a desk with a typewriter in front of us. I frown as I stare at it, where did he get this photo?

"Anderson Media is the brainchild of Wade Anderson." He gestures to Fletch. "Fletcher's father, who along with his wife, our beloved Claire Anderson, started this company from a one-room office. They worked hard with blood, sweat and tears to create the wonderful company that is here and still standing today." He paces back and forth across the stage as he talks, he clicks the remote and photos from the early Anderson Media days come up on the screen.

"As you all know, tragedy struck six years ago when Wade Anderson was killed in a bike accident." He walks around as he talks. "Since that time, Anderson Media has suffered a chain of serious losses. Though none as great as the personal loss of Wade."

My eyes well with tears as I watch Fletcher sitting on the stage, his back is straight as he crosses his legs, he's detached from the situation. It's obvious to me that Tristan has read him this speech before, it's not the first time he's heard it.

"So why am I here?" He continues to pace. "The company is floundering."

The room is silent, hanging off his every word.

"I have an invested interest in protecting it for Wade's sons." He gestures to Fletcher on the stage. "Who, one day, will inherit this company."

He clicks the remote and a photograph of my three boys comes up onto the screen.

"Anderson Media is returning to the forefront of where it should be. I have resigned from Miles Media and will be taking over as the new CEO."

The room gasps.

"Why, you ask?

"I am engaged to Claire Anderson, and her boys...will soon be my stepsons."

Louder gasps.

Marley elbows me and I smirk, they don't know how the hell I managed to snag this guy...neither do I, actually. It's a shock to me too, people.

"Anyone who knows me, knows one thing. Family is everything." He continues to pace. "Anderson Media belongs to my sons, therefore I am going to do everything in my power to protect and grow it." He looks out over the crowd. "It's not going to be easy, many of you will not make it. You will not be able to cope with the transition and I understand that. Change is uncomfortable." He continues to pace,

"Tomorrow you are all going to apply for a new role within the company. Nobody is staying in their current position. You are all too comfortable and set in your ways."

The room is silent, hanging on his every word.

"You will have new KPIs, budgets and targets, and yes there will be pressure to perform."

Hushed whispers of horror sound throughout the audience.

"But along with that, there will be a pay increase, an incentive bonus structure and many opportunities to shine."

The audience is getting noisy now.

He holds up his hands to quieten everyone down, and once they finally quieten, he continues.

"I ask one thing of you all. Do not waste my time. Go home tonight and make a decision. Do you want to work harder than you ever have before, or do you want to resign immediately? We don't have time to train those who don't want to be here, and we completely understand if you don't." He continues to pace. "Some of you may already know your decision and I will be accepting email resignations. You don't even have to come back tomorrow; all severance pay will be honored in full."

"If you stay, know one thing." He stops and looks out into the audience, "I do not accept laziness, I have high expectations and demand the best. Because that's what I give."

My heart swells with pride. *I love this man.*

"I will now call on our new GM, Fletcher Anderson, to address you."

It's me who gasps this time, he's named Fletcher as the General Manager.

What the fuck?

"Thank you, Tristan." Fletcher takes the microphone

from him. "Hello." He smiles out to the audience. "Thank you all for coming."

I sit back in my chair as I listen to Fletcher talk with such an easy confidence with tears in my eyes, knowing that Wade is looking down on this day with so much pride for his son.

I'm blown away.

It's 5 p.m. and I make my way into the CEO's office.

"Knock, knock."

"Come in," Tristan calls without looking up.

"Hi."

He glances up and then smiles warmly. "Hey."

I slide an envelope over the desk to him. "I came to bring you this."

He raises his eyebrow.

"It's my resignation."

"Why?" He frowns.

"Because you and Fletch have everything handled here." I put my hand over my stomach. "Because I want to concentrate on our baby and being a mom."

His eyes search mine.

"It's better this way, Tris. You handle work." I put his hand over my stomach. "And let me handle this."

He pulls me down onto his lap and I kiss him softly. "I love you."

"I don't want to push you out." He sighs.

"You haven't, sweetheart. You've set me free."

———

"Claire," Marley calls in her singsong voice, "someone's at the door for you."

I come around the corner to the hugest bunch of red roses I've ever seen, my mouth falls open in surprise. "My god."

"Sign here." The delivery man smiles as he leans up onto his toes. "Somebody sure loves you."

I sign his delivery pad as I beam with happiness.

"She's getting married today," Marley announces proudly. "To a god."

"Well." The delivery man laughs. "Lucky you."

"I am." I take the flowers from him. "Thank you. Have a nice day."

"Good luck today." He smiles.

"Thanks." Suddenly I'm all emotional and I kiss him on the cheek. "And thanks for my flowers."

"You're welcome, but I have to tell you. They aren't from me."

I laugh, embarrassed, why did I just kiss him on the cheek?

"Bye." Marley closes the door and I breeze through my house. "I don't think I've got a vase big enough for these." I lay them onto the kitchen counter and unpin the card.

I can't wait to marry you today
Forever mine.
Tristan.
XO

I swoon as I hold the card to my chest.

This man.

"Give me that." Marley snatches the card from me and reads it out loud. "I can't wait to marry you today. Forever mine. Tristan." She rolls her eyes in a dramatic fashion. "Oh my god, could he be any more fucking perfect?" She sighs dreamily.

I smile as I continue to look for a vase.

"Seriously?" Marley continues. "Forever his. Fuck my life." She looks up at the sky and shakes her fist. "Where is my Tristan, God? How come Claire gets one and I don't?"

I inhale their deep perfume. I know exactly how I have a Tristan and nobody else does. Wade sent him, there isn't a doubt in my mind that the stars had already been aligned in heaven.

It's been a weird week, weird month, actually.

We've hit the ground running, a lot has happened, I fell pregnant, got engaged. Tristan was hell-bent on being married before the baby is born and I didn't want to be a huge bride.

So we had precisely four weeks to pull together a wedding, plus I've had morning sickness from hell. No idea where it's come from, I wasn't sick at all with the boys.

This older pregnancy thing is not for the fainthearted, let me tell you.

Thankfully, Tristan has taken care of almost every detail. Who knew wedding planning would be his thing?

Marley takes the flowers from me. "I'll find a vase for these, you need to start getting ready."

"Is this really happening, Mol?"

"Uh-uh," She nods. "You have bagged the biggest, sweetest hunk in the world."

"I have, haven't I?" I hunch my shoulders up in excitement. "I wonder what's going on with the boys?"

We are marrying in the church that Tristan's parents married in in New York. The boys are at his penthouse getting ready together. I wanted them to stay here but he wanted to stick with the *no seeing the bride the night before* tradition.

"Knowing Tristan, he will be all drill sergeant over there making sure everything is running to schedule, the boys will all be in their suits and being warned with death if they get dirty." Marley smirks as she fills the vase.

"He would, wouldn't he. That's exactly how it would be going." I smile. "I still can't believe he asked the three boys to be his groomsmen."

"Why not?"

"He has three brothers who are his best friends, and yet he asked the boys to stand beside him."

"Because he's Tristan." Marley widens her eyes. "Need I say more."

"This is true." I turn and float up the hallway to my bedroom, I rub my hand over my small baby bump.

Forever his.

Tristan

Jameson holds up his glass of champagne. "A toast."

I smile and raise my glass to his, Christopher and Elliot do the same.

Dressed in black dinner suits, we are primped and primed for my wedding day.

"To happiness."

The silhouettes of my beloved brothers blur as emotion overwhelms me.

"Fuck me dead, if you cry like a baby at this wedding..." Jameson mutters dryly.

"As if he won't," Elliot replies. "Please, save me the drama."

We all laugh and I shake my head in disbelief. "Who the hell am I these days?"

"Maybe you're pregnant too?" Christopher winks.

"Fuck off."

We're out on the terrace of my penthouse, as hungover as all fuck. What was supposed to be a quiet night with my boys ended up in a rowdy card game with my brothers as well. They ended up all staying here and I don't know what happened, one minute we were playing cards and then Jameson brought out a case of Dalmore Scotch, next minute, all seven of us were dancing on the furniture.

Even Patrick.

I look in at the boys as they play PlayStation. "You reckon it's late enough for them to get dressed yet?"

"They can't get dirty now, surely?" Jameson shrugs.

"You'd be surprised." I glance at my watch. "Yeah it's getting close, we leave in just over an hour." I stick my head in through the glass doors. "Start getting ready, boys."

"Yes, finally." Patrick drops the remote like a hot potato and runs upstairs at full speed.

"I think he's excited." Elliot smiles.

"I fucking love that kid," Christopher says as he watches him disappear out of view. "I'm excited too."

I drain my glass of champagne. "I'm going to go and help them." I pat my suit pockets. "Jay, you've got the rings, right?"

He pats his jacket inside pocket to check. "Yep."

"Elliot?" I ask.

Elliot pulls out folded pieces of paper from his pocket. "Got the speeches."

"Christopher?" I ask him.

"I know, I know. No photos." He ticks his finger. "Check, check, double fucking check, if I see a phone I'm going ham."

I don't want any details of the wedding to leak to the press, it's just not happening.

"Okay." My brothers may not be acting as my official groomsmen in the church, but they are unofficially still my groomsmen.

I couldn't do this without them.

"Okay, I'm getting the boys ready." I slap Jameson on the back as I walk past him into the house. "Back soon."

I take the stairs and walk down the hall; Patrick is in one bathroom showering and Fletcher is in another I find Harry lying on his bed in his room. "How come you aren't in the shower?" I ask him.

"I was thinking." He scrunches his pillow up and rolls it under his head as he lies on his back as if he has all the time in the world.

Fuck me, not now.

"About what?" I take his suit bag from his wardrobe and hang it from the door.

"I think I need to shave today...you know, for the wedding."

My eyes flick over to him, he doesn't have one fucking whisker. "Do you now?"

"Yeah."

"Okay." I throw my hands out and gesture to the bathroom. "So go shave."

"Yeah but..." he continues, "...it's going to take time."

"So don't get any ideas about shaving your two pubes, we are in a hurry today."

"Why would I shave my pubes?" He frowns.

"I don't know. Why do you do any of the weird shit you do?" I throw a towel at him. "Get up."

He exhales heavily and drags himself into the bathroom and closes the door.

Seriously....

I hear Patrick's shower turn off and I walk into his bedroom, his suit is already laid out on his bed and I smile as I look over it. His bathroom door opens and he appears with a towel around his waist. I go to his wardrobe and grab a bottle of deodorant and pass it over to him. "Wear deodorant today."

He looks at it in his hand and then back up at me. "Why, I'm just a kid. I don't sweat."

"I'm not taking any chances. You will smell nice today if it kills you."

"Okay then." He rolls his eyes in an overdramatic way. "Fine."

"Call me when you're dressed and I'll do your tie."

"Okay."

"And don't forget your vest," I remind him as I walk out of the room, I head down to Fletcher. His bedroom is at the end of the hall, I find him already dressed in his suit and doing his tie in the mirror, I feel myself relax a little bit. "That's my boy." I slap him on the back as he looks in the mirror at himself. "Do I look okay?" he asks.

"You look great, man." I take over doing his tie for him.

He gives me a proud smile. "I do, don't I?"

"Argh," We hear a cry come from Harry's room. "Tristan."

"Fuck's sake, what now?" I whisper as I march down the hall.

Harry has a towel around his waist, the hot water is running and the bathroom is full of steam. He is holding a flannel to his face and there is blood everywhere.

"What the fuck is happening in here?" I gasp.

"I nicked myself shaving."

I lift the flannel back to see a huge laceration to his lip and my eyes bulge. "You shaved your lip? In what universe do you shave your fucking lip? You don't shave a lip, nobody shaves a lip. Everybody knows you don't shave a fucking lip."

"I don't know." He shrugs. "Stop saying lip."

My god.

"We do not have time for this shit today, Harrison." I tear a tiny bit of toilet paper and put it on the cut.

"Argh," He winces.

"Do not talk." I press on the toilet paper hard. "You do not have whiskers on your face, let alone your fucking lip. Hold that on there and it will stop bleeding in a moment, it's just a nick."

Is it though?

I can feel my temperature rising by the second.

Why?

"Do not put your white shirt on until it stops bleeding, do you understand me?" I warn him.

"Yes."

"So what are you going to do now?" I ask him to make sure.

"Get in the shower and wash my hair."

"You haven't showered yet?"

"No."

I inhale deeply, this kid kills me.

"Okay, shower, I'm going downstairs. Call me when you are ready to dress so I can check the cut."

I march back downstairs to find my three brothers relaxing happily on the terrace. "Give me a drink," I whisper as I pick up my glass of champagne.

"What's going on up there?" Jameson asks.

"Harrison shaved and nearly cut his lip off, that's what's going on. Looks like a fucking chainsaw massacre up there."

"Jesus Christ," Jameson mutters.

Elliot's face falls. "Is he alright?"

"I don't know."

"I'm going to check on him." Elliot bounds inside and disappears up the stairs.

I exhale heavily as I try to calm myself down. "It's fine."

"There's heaps of blood?" Jameson frowns.

"Yep."

"I cut my balls shaving them once, thought I was going to need a transfusion," Christopher replies casually into his drink.

"You shave your balls?" Jameson frowns over at him.

"Yeah. Don't you?" Christopher fires back.

"Stop talking about balls," I snap, cutting them off. "I just want today to go smoothly."

"It will, relax," Christopher replies.

"Ahh...Tristan," Elliot's voice calls from inside. "We have a new problem."

I glance inside.

"An even bigger one," he calls again. "You might need to come in here."

"Fuck me, what now?" I glance inside to see Harry standing awkwardly at the bottom of the stairs, the blood drains from my face.

His suit is four sizes too small. The sleeves are midway up his forearms and the trouser pants are halfway up his shins. He can hardly move in it at all.

"What the fuck is that shit?" I cry.

Jameson and Christopher start to laugh from behind me.

"I asked you to try your suit on last *Wednesday* when it arrived and you told me it fits..." I cry in an outrage. "You lied about trying it on?"

"I didn't get around to it yet," he fires back.

"Didn't get around to it, I tell you what I'm about to get around to, Harrison...ending you," I yell as I glance at my watch. "This is a disaster."

Christopher and Jameson are laughing hard now.

"Shut the fuck up, you two," I yell.

"It's fine." Elliot calmly takes out his phone, "I'm calling the seamstress now, they can deliver another suit. We have time. They have heaps of the same suits there. It's going to be fine." He smiles to Harry. "It's all fine."

This is as far from fine as physically possible.

I begin to pace as Jameson and Christopher continue to snicker between themselves. I turn toward them, infuriated. "Unless you two want to be murdered, I would strongly advise you to shut your mouths."

"We will if we get around to it," Christopher replies like the smart-ass he is, Jameson bursts out laughing again.

I hold my temples; I do not need this shit from these assholes today.

"Okay, well when will that be?" Elliot's eyes flick to me as he listens. "Well that's not good enough, the wedding is in an hour." He fakes a smile as he listens again and I know that look, the psychotic part of his brain is just about to be activated. "I understand that you said to try it on when we got it. However, that didn't happen." His eyes flick up to Harry and he puts his finger up and pretends to slice his throat.

Harry smiles, his eyes twinkling with mischief.

Don't smile, fucker.

"What size is the suit?" Elliot asks.

Jameson takes the jacket off Harry and looks at the label. "It's a thirty-two."

"Thirty-two," Elliot replies to the person on the phone. "That's the right size?" He frowns. "Impossible. He hasn't grown that much in three weeks; he isn't the fucking Hulk, Janet."

Christopher and Jameson burst out laughing and I tip my head back and drain my glass. "This is unbelievable."

"We are on our way down now," Elliot snaps. "You have every suit size ready and waiting." He hangs up. "Get in the car."

"What?" My eyes widen.

"We've got to go to the suit place."

"What? Now?" I gasp. "We don't have time."

"We don't have time to call for the car, but if we drive ourselves we'll make it. We'll go straight to the church from the suit shop. I'll drive. It's fine, I've totally got this," Elliot replies.

"Elliot is right, it is fine. Stop wasting time and let's go," Christopher replies.

"I wanted a relaxing wedding day," I scream. "Can anything ever run smoothly around here?"

Jameson and Christopher begin to round everyone up in a whirlwind and five minutes later we are all in the elevator. I glance over to Fletcher; he looks like he just crawled out of a dumpster. "Did you even do your hair?"

"I didn't have time," he gasps.

"You look like a hobo," I whisper angrily.

"I forgot to put on deodorant," Patrick chimes in.

I close my eyes to stop myself from speaking...or yelling...or swearing.

Fainting for that matter.

All the swear words are on the tip of my tongue...and then some new ones that haven't even been discovered yet.

Jameson's shoulders bounce as he tries to hold in his giggles.

The elevator doors open and everyone runs for the car. "Put the back seats up," I yell.

"Okay."

"Patrick and Fletch, climb into the back."

I pop the trunk and they climb into the back seat and fold the extra seats up, two minutes later we are flying out of the parking lot. Elliot is driving, Jameson is the navigator, Christopher, Harry and I are in the back seat and Tricky and Fletch are squeezed into the back row.

"Left," Jameson says, Elliot turns to the left. "I mean right." Elliot swerves the car to the right.

"Ahhh," We all hang on for dear life as Elliot speeds down the street.

"Slow down," Christopher yells. "I want to make it there alive; you know."

"If we don't make it there on time, I'll be driving us over a cliff," I announce as I run my hands through my hair. "I hope you are all prepared for that."

"There are no cliffs in New York," Harry replies sarcastically.

"Bridge," I sneer through gritted teeth. "A big, huge, giant fucking bridge." I crack my knuckles.

So help me god, this kid might actually die today.

"It says here turn left," Jameson says as he reads the maps on his phone. "But I know a shortcut."

"Oh my god," the car collectively screams. "No, don't do it."

"Don't listen to him," Christopher snaps. "Follow the maps."

"Trust me on this."

"You do not know a fucking shortcut. You have a driver everywhere you go," I call.

"My driver knows shortcuts," he barks.

"Your driver isn't here," we all cry in unison again.

Christopher leans over and snatches the phone from Jameson. "Turn left," he yells.

Elliot screeches the tires as he makes a sharp left. "Ahhh." We all hang on for dear life.

"Do you have your seat belts on in the back?" I call.

"Yes," replies Fletcher. "Patrick doesn't."

"What?" I turn my head to see Patrick fussing around with his seat belt. "What are you doing back there?"

"It won't." He struggles some more. "It won't click in."

"Help him," I yell to Fletcher. "Why are you just sitting there?"

"Left," Christopher yells, the car screams around the corner at speed and we all hang on again. "Right up here."

We slow down behind a queue of traffic and I drag my hand down my face. "This is not what I had in mind, Harrison."

He smiles goofily up at me and puts his hand on my thigh. "But it's fun, right?"

"No," the whole car cries.

Unable to help it, I smirk. "Maybe a little bit."

We maneuver through the city and I glance at my watch. "The wedding starts in forty minutes. We'll never make it!"

"It's just up here around the corner," Christopher cries.

"Where will I park?" Elliot calls as he grips the steering wheel. "Oh no, it's a one-way street."

"This is the most fucking stressful day of my life," Jameson yells, he opens the glove box in search of something. "Bingo." He pulls out a can of deodorant and undoes his shirt and sprays it on. "I'm sweating like a pig."

"Pass it back here," I yell.

"Don't use it all, I don't have any on in the first place," Patrick calls from the back seat.

"Because you're a kid," Jameson growls.

The deodorant gets passed around the car as we all put it on in a mad fluster.

"I don't know where to park," Elliot yells. "There's nowhere to park."

"Just pull over, we will get out. Circle the block a few times." I undo my seat belt. "Boys, you are all coming with me."

"What?" Fletcher replies. "Shouldn't we stay in the car?"

"We stay together," I yell. "Out of the fucking car right now."

The car pulls up and I jump out, Harrison next, and the two boys in the back seat dive over the seat in a chaotic mess of arms and legs. The car behind us beeps its horn. "Shut up," Jameson bellows out the window as he slaps his hand on the side of the car. "Don't make me come back there."

"Where is it?" I yell to Christopher through the window.

"Around the corner to the left."

I grab Patrick's hand. "Run." We take off up the street like maniacs.

"My shoes are hurting me," Harrison yells.

"Not as badly as I want to," I yell back, I glance at my watch. "Half an hour." I speed up. "Faster."

We finally arrive at the suit shop, push the door open panting messes, and the lady smiles calmly. "Hello."

"Hi." I pant and point to Harry. "Suit."

She looks him up and down. "Hmm, it doesn't fit whatsoever, does it?"

"No." I fume, I glance at my watch. "We have to be at the church in twenty-six minutes. *Hurry up.*"

Her face pales. "Oh dear. This way, I have them all laid out for you."

Harry and she disappear into a changing room and the boys and I all fix our hair in the reflection in the window. I try to smooth Patrick's hair and fix his tie, I neaten Fletcher and then myself, I glance at my watch. "Hurry up," I yell. "We have twenty-one minutes to get to the church."

"Ta-da." Harry appears and holds his hands out like he's a magician in a perfectly fitted suit.

"I'll ta-da you alright," I fume. "Let's go."

"I'll just…" the woman from the shop says as she goes to her computer.

"Not now," I yell as we run out of the shop, I look up and down the street. "Where are they?"

"I can't see them." Fletcher cranes his neck.

I go to dial Jameson's number and a cab pulls up in front of us. "Get in."

"What?"

"Get in the cab, we will meet them at the church." We all dive in the cab.

"Where to?" the bored cab driver asks.

"St Patrick's Cathedral. We have eighteen minutes to get there and I'm the fucking groom. Drive it like you stole it."

The cab driver's eyes widen and he pulls out at speed into the traffic.

I text Jameson,

MEET US AT THE CHURCH,
WE ARE IN A CAB.

I glance at my watch, fourteen minutes.
Fuck.

Claire.

Dad holds my hand as we drive in the car, we are on our way to the church. I'm not sure if it's being pregnant or what but I'm feeling overemotional. Like the whole entirety of my being is about to be played out.

It's my wedding day.

My second wedding day.

A day that I never imagined doing twice.

I stare out the car window with my mind in a whirlwind, flicking between time zones. Reminiscing from my last wedding…. my last groom, to this life and this man.

Loving my new husband-to-be so deeply that I don't have the words to describe it.

Two men, two very different loves.

One, my childhood sweetheart, the only man I knew, and we had all our firsts together. The father of my children, our love was easy and uncomplicated. Everything to achieve and nothing to prove.

And then there's Tristan, my beautiful, gorgeous Tristan.

Our love is deep, so deep that I don't know how I could have ever lived a life without his love. And looking back, I don't think I was meant to.

We were always going to meet, always going to be together.

Tristan's love brought me back to life, brought my children back to life. He will never ever know the depths of my love and appreciation for him.

He had the world at his feet and yet, he fell in love with me. Never once did he falter, never once did he miss a step. Rock sturdy, the love of our lives.

I put my hand over my stomach and smile wistfully out the window. *Our baby.*

A celebration of the two of us.

"Are you okay, love?" Dad asks.

Am I okay?

"I'm more than okay, Dad." I smile broadly. "I'm great." The car slowly pulls to a stop out the front of the church and I glance down at myself. "Do I look okay?"

"You look so beautiful. He's a very lucky man."

I'm wearing a cream lace fitted wedding gown, complete with full veil. I would have been happy to get married in a registry office but Tristan wanted the whole shebang.

So here I am, pregnant and dressed in a traditional wedding dress.

A cab pulls up across the road and the four doors all swing open at the same time. "What's...."

Fletcher jumps out and then Harrison.

"What in the world?" I frown.

Tristan appears and drags Patrick out by the hand; he nearly pulls his arm out the socket.

Like maniacs they run across the road dressed in their suits and disappear into the church.

Dad and I look at each other and then back at them. "What in the world?"

"I have no idea." Dad shrugs.

Suddenly Tristan's car pulls up and Jameson, Elliot and Christopher dive out, also dressed in black tie, and sprint into the church.

I burst out laughing, only us. I don't know what's happened but I'm pretty sure Tristan would be stressed out to the max.

The driver goes to open my door.

I wind down the window. "I just want to wait a few moments if that's okay?"

"Of course." He stands back.

We sit in the car for a bit and Dad twists his lips. "What do you reckon made them so late?"

We both burst out laughing. "God only knows."

Marley and the bridesmaids catch sight of us and come bounding over to the car. "Come on. Come on."

"Okay." I beam. "Let's do this."

. . .

The traditional bridal waltz echoes through the church and I watch on as Marley, then Melanie and Samantha, my cousins, walk down the aisle in front of me.

The church is decorated with beautiful white flowers in the most over-the-top grandeur. Tristan has thought of every little detail and planned this wedding to perfection.

With a lump in my throat Dad and I make our way down the aisle, and then I see him.

Them.

My four boys all lined up in a row.

My entire heart and everything in between.

Black dinner suits, disheveled hair, their smiles so big that they could light up space.

Patrick is bouncing on the end in excitement.

But it's Tristan that I'm fixed on.

His eyes sparkle with that certain something and the look he gives me is pure mischief, he's biting his lip and goes up onto his toes in excitement.

I get the giggles as I get closer, and so does he. Everyone in the church does too.

This is unbelievable.

Never in a million years when we had that first meeting could we have ever imagined this.

And yet here we are.

We get to the altar and Dad kisses me on both cheeks and shakes Tristan's hand.

"Anderson." Tristan smiles mischievously.

It makes me giggle, I thought he would be all emotional today, but it actually makes more sense that he would be his playful sexy self.

He takes me into his arms and with his hands on my behind he kisses me, a little bit too much actually.

"Ease up," Christopher calls and the church all laugh again.

He smiles against my lips and whispers, "Let's fucking do this."

Three months later.

The removalist truck pulls into the street as we follow in the car, Tristan, Patrick and Harry are in Tristan's car in front of us. Fletcher and I are loaded to the brim, Woofy and Muff in the back seat, and today's the day that we move into our new home. The truck pulls into the driveway and we all pull our cars over.

Tristan bounds out of the car and holds his hands up like he's some crazy game-show host. "And here she is," he yells in an over-the-top animated voice. "Home sweet home."

"Oh my god, he's so embarrassing," Fletcher mutters under his breath as he looks around at the neighbors' houses.

I giggle as I climb out of the car. "You got that right."

I stare up at the house in awe, it's so beautiful. Huge and grand, with a lived-in family feel. Seven bedrooms, a study. A pool, you name it, this house has it.

Tristan and I came to an agreement, we kept our old house and one day it will be the boys'. For the next few years we are going to rent it out. It's the perfect scenario, the house stays with us, but we get to move into a bigger place. I'm not going to lie, having more room is going to be amazing, especially with the baby coming.

The removalists begin to open the back of the truck as they get sorted and Fletcher grabs Woofy's lead and Harry grabs Muff's cat carrier cage. Patrick carries the beloved rocket model, they didn't trust that with the removal van.

Tristan goes through the keys as he walks up onto the veranda. "Mrs. Miles." He holds his arm out for me. "Come here, please."

Harry and Patrick roll their eyes at each other and I smile and walk up onto the veranda beside him.

"It is customary for the man of the house to carry the woman of the house over the threshold for the first time."

"Better let me do it then," Harry announces.

The boys snicker.

Tristan gives him the side eye. "Move aside," he says, he goes to pick me up and struggles with a grunt. "Argh." He steps backward and struggles some more.

"What's the problem, man of the house?" I roll my lips to hide my smile, a six-month-pregnant woman is no lightweight.

"Don't worry, Anderson." He grunts as he swings me up. "I've got this. My sheer brute strength makes you light as a feather."

"Liar." I giggle as I hang on for dear life, I really thought after we got married, he would never call me Anderson ever again. Glad to report that I was wrong, some things never change.

His step falters once more as he carries me like a bride.

"You're weak as water." Harrison rolls his eyes. "Wimp."

"Apparently," Tristan winces with a strained voice. "Move out of the way."

"Don't you dare drop her," Fletcher warns. "There's a baby inside."

"Out of the way then," Tristan fires back with a sense of urgency.

We walk through the front door and he slides me down his body, with his arms around me he kisses me softly. "Welcome home, sweetheart." His lips linger over mine as he puts his hand protectively over my pregnant stomach. "I love you."

I smile up at my beautiful husband. "I love you more."

"Oh god, here they go again," Harrison moans.

"Tris...." I look around at the grand foyer. "I can't believe this house is really ours."

"Only the best for my family." Tristan smiles proudly with his hands on his hips. "Anyone leave any shoes at the front door and it's go time," he adds.

The removalists carry the first piece of furniture up the front lawn. "Where do you want this?"

"Upstairs." He takes the stairs two at a time like an excited little kid. "This way."

———

"The baby is now the size of a large cantaloupe," Tristan calls, he's deep in concentration, lying on the couch with his feet up over the back of it.

Fletcher rolls his eyes at me as I toss the salad.

"Really?" I call.

"Yeah, and did you know that it can now distinguish voices and sounds?"

"Really?" I call again as I smile, I did know that but I'll let him tell me.

"So we better start talking more to her, boys," he calls again.

"Why do you keep calling it a her?" I ask.

"I have a feeling," he calls back. "So everyone start talking to Mom's stomach more."

Harry walks through the kitchen, he bends down to my stomach in an overexaggerated way. "Your father is annoying," he tells it.

I giggle and cup Harry's face. "Little bit."

"I heard that," Tristan calls again.

Tristan Miles has a new hobby, reading pregnancy books out loud to us all, telling us random facts that we really don't need to know.

He is studying all things baby.

"We're going, Mom," Fletcher says.

"What time will you be back?"

"A few hours."

"Okay." I smile, Harrison has basketball practice and Fletcher wants to take him, it seems Fletch is a bit sweet on the assistant coach. Trinity College has been a godsend for Harry. He's in the debating and basketball team, he has a heap of new friends and apparently a hot assistant basketball coach.

"Bye Tris," they call as they head out the door.

"Drive carefully," he calls back.

We hear the car start and pull away and I smile, I give it five minutes.

I feel two hands slink around my waist from behind and I giggle. "Five seconds?"

"What is?" He kisses me softly, the need behind his lips is as clear as day.

"I said to myself that I give it five minutes until you are out here with me and it was five seconds instead."

He kisses me deeper, his tongue sliding against mine, my man is hungry...and not for the salad I'm making.

"What do you want, Daddy?" I smile against his lips.

He puts his two hands on the sides of my stomach. "Cover

your ears," he tells the baby before kissing me again. "Daddy needs to fuck," he breathes.

I giggle, good lord, we cannot get enough of each other. Every chance we get we are at it like rabbits.

He is obsessed with my body as it changes.

He moves his hand up my thigh and slips his fingers into my panties, he slides his fingers through my wet flesh and inhales sharply. "You need to be punished." He pushes a finger deep inside me and I clench around him. "I do." He pumps me with it and I spread my legs a little to give him greater access.

"Get to bed," he growls.

"Patrick is going to be home any minute."

"Then fucking hurry up," he snaps, he grabs my hand and pulls me up the stairs and marches me down the hallway to our bedroom, once inside he flicks the lock and turns toward me.

We stare at each other, so much magic between us and yet when we are like this, only one thing matters.

Touch.

He goes to take my dress off over my head.

"We don't have time for that," I snap. "Just fuck me."

He bends and takes my panties off and then points to the bed. "Get on your hands and knees."

Excitement runs through me and I kneel on the side of the bed.

His fingers run through my flesh and he lets out a low whistle. "You have no fucking idea how hot you are like this."

I giggle and then he grabs my hip bones and slams in hard, knocking the air from my lungs, holding himself deep.

My body ripples around him as it adjusts to his size.

In the beginning of my pregnancy Tristan was scared he

was going to hurt the baby, but now...now he's back to his bad boy self and I fucking love it.

He fucks me, deep and hard, and I can feel every vein on his thick engorged length as it hits just the right spot.

A car pulls up out the front. "Patrick is home."

"Fuck it." He pumps me harder, fast and furious. Chasing the release that we both need.

"So good," I breathe.

He pushes my shoulders down to the bed with his hands and the change in position sends me spiraling headfirst into a killer of an orgasm, I moan into the mattress and he slams once...

Twice.

Three times, and holds himself deep as he comes into my body.

The front door slams shut. "Tristan, Mom?" Patrick calls from downstairs.

"Fuck it." He pulls out and quickly kisses my behind and then slaps it. "Got to go." He puts his shorts on and runs to the door and disappears. "Coming, buddy," he calls as I hear him run down the stairs. "How was it?"

He knows that if he doesn't go find Patrick, Patrick will come looking for us.

He's giving me time to get myself together.

I smile into my pillow, my heart is still racing, my body quivering all over.

I need all the time.

Orgasmic relaxation is beginning to float in.

I'm taking a nap.

Tristan sits on the floor as he reads the instructions again. "No. that doesn't make sense."

"Give me that." Harry snatches the instructions from him.

"I'm telling you that the wheels go on first," Fletcher replies.

"Who wrote these instructions anyway?" Tristan huffs. "I'm sick of these idiots who can't write instructions."

"Maybe the people who can't read them are the idiots." I widen my eyes.

He fakes a smile and then drops his face deadpan.

Patrick holds up the bag of screws as he inspects them.

"Don't lose those, Tricky."

I watch from the rocking chair in the corner, the boys are in the nursery attempting to build the pram.

Attempting being the key word.

They built the cradle yesterday and the cot this morning, but this stroller has got them stumped.

"Are there any more instructions?" Tristan asks, distracted. "Surely that can't be it."

"When I get a hold of this guy," Harry fumes, he punches his fist for added effect.

"Maybe we got some in that other envelope, I'll go look." I walk down to my bedroom and grab the paperwork and walk back to the nursery. "Here try this." I pass it to Tristan.

He begins reading and frowns. "What's this?"

"It's the court papers."

"For what?"

"For the adoption hearing."

His eyes rise to meet mine.

"It's time," I whisper.

The boys gasp.

He blinks back tears. "What?"

"I want you to be the boy's father." I smile hopefully. "Legally. Before the baby comes."

I secretly lodged the papers months ago and they have only just been approved.

He reads the papers as if unable to believe it and his face screws up in emotion.

"Look what you did, Harry," Patrick snaps outraged. "He's crying now because he has to be your father and you're so naughty. Harry is going to be good from now on, aren't you, Harry."

Tristan pulls Patrick onto his lap. "They're happy tears, Tricky." He holds his arms out for the other boys. "Come here."

"Stacks on," Harry yells.

The boys all dive on Tristan and they all laugh and hug as they roll around on the floor. "I love you brats."

"We love you too."

Tears fill my eyes as I watch them, they are so close.

Wade would want this for his sons, to have a father who loves them with all of his heart. To give them what he no longer can.

The lump in my throat is so big that it hurts.

This is the right thing.

———

"All rise." The judge walks into the family law court and the room stands.

We sit in the front row, all five of us.

Tristan is beaming with happiness, the children too. Dressed in their best suits, I think they are all more excited than when we got married.

This is a big deal to them.

And to me.

In my pregnant state I'm feeling overemotional. There have been lots of tears, happy tears. But when I saw Wade's parents walk in quietly and sit at the back of the courtroom my heart broke a little.

It means a lot that they are here to support me and the kids with this. They adore Tristan and know this is what Wade would have wanted. It's what's best for the boys, I know it too, but it's just all a little real today.

Jameson and Emily, Elliot and Christopher are all here, as are Tristan's parents, my parents and brother.

It's a big day for our family.

The judge has gray hair and is wearing a robe, he looks over the top of his gold-rimmed glasses and smiles at us with a kind nod, he then looks down at the paperwork in front of him. "I'm here today to call on the matter of adoption of Fletcher Anderson, Harrison Anderson, and Patrick Anderson."

The room sits quietly and Tristan squeezes my hand in his.

"Mr. Miles, you have filled out the appropriate paperwork?" he asks as he looks over a pile of papers in front of him.

"Yes, Your Honor." Tristan squeezes my hand again.

"I have reviewed the file and believe that it is in the best interest of Fletcher, Harrison and Patrick Anderson to be adopted by Tristan Miles."

The boys all beam with excitement and I smile as I watch them, they are nearly jumping out of their seats and can hardly sit still.

"Firstly we will sign the adoption agreement. Parents are

to sign and any child over the age of fourteen will sign for themselves." He passes the paperwork to the secretary. "You may sign now." Tristan and I and Fletcher stand and sign where we are told to.

Christopher is snapping away taking photos with his phone.

We sign where we are told and the secretary checks our signatures and hands the papers back to the judge, he reads them over the top of his glasses. "By signing this document I hereby declare that you, Tristan Miles, are now a parent under the eyes of law. You will have all rights and duties of the parent-child relationship but most importantly all of the joys."

Tristan smiles broadly down at the boys.

"Congratulations, Mr. Miles." He bangs his hammer. "May you all be a very happy family."

He gets up and walks out of the room and Tristan and the boys hug.

Everyone shakes his hand and hugs the boys and I glance over to Wade's parents who are still sitting in the back row.

I'm glad they came, I really am.

They eventually make their way down to us and Tristan turns and shakes Wade's father's hand and kisses his mother on the cheek. "Thank you so much for coming. It means a lot."

"Wade would have wanted us here."

And the tears come, filling my eyes with love and sadness and memories and hope.

Wade's mom pulls me in for a hug as I try to pull myself together, she gets it.

I'm sad for Wade, but happy for the boys.

"We're having afternoon tea back at our house," Tristan says to them. "We would love it if you could join us."

"That would be lovely." Frank nods. "We will meet you there." With one more hug for the boys from everyone, we make our way back out to the parking lot and all climb in the car. "So what do we call you now?" Harrison asks from the back seat.

Tristan's eyes flick up to him in the rearview mirror. "Whatever you want to call me."

"Donkey," Harrison asks.

I giggle, if only they knew how much that suits him.

"Not Donkey." Tristan rolls his eyes.

"Well if I can't call you Donkey, I'm calling you Dad," Harry says.

"Okay...." Tristan's nostrils flare as he keeps his eyes on the road. "Dad it is."

"Can I call you Daddy?" I tease.

Tristan's eyes flick over to me and then drop down to my breasts.

Dirty bastard.

"He's not your daddy, Mom," Patrick announces. "He's ours, you already have a dad."

Tristan chuckles and picks up my hand and kisses my fingertips.

"Oh for god's sake, concentrate on the road," Harry moans.

Two months later.

"You call me tonight and check in," Tristan tells Fletcher.

"Yes."

"And I don't want you driving after ten at night."

Fletcher rolls his eyes.

"Actually, don't go out at all until we get back. It's just a week, it won't hurt you to stay at home with your brothers. You are in charge of the house, stay here and concentrate on that."

"Dad." Fletcher moans. "Stop."

"I just don't....." Tristan turns back to me. "Maybe this isn't a good time to go away, Claire."

"We are *going*." I widen my eyes at him. "I want some time alone with my husband."

Tristan exhales heavily as if I'm the biggest inconvenience in the world and looks back to the boys who are lined up in a row to say goodbye. We are going away for a week before the baby is born, Mom and Dad are here to stay with the kids.

We booked it back when we first got married but now that it's come around, Tristan is frantic about leaving the boys, this is the first time he's had to do it.

Tristan moves to Harrison. "Harry, now...." He pauses as he thinks for a moment. "You know what is going to happen if you get into trouble while we are gone, don't you?"

"Yes." Harry nods.

"And is it going to be worth it?"

"No, Dad."

"And you are in charge of what?"

"Cleaning the pool and mowing the lawn."

Tristan nods and hugs him. "Right, look after your grandparents, please. And no gaming after nine."

I smirk as I watch on.

He moves to Patrick. "Okay, Tricky, you are in charge of the animals and watering the garden."

"I know." Patrick smiles proudly.

"And helping Gran."

"I know."

"And you can ring us anytime. You know that don't you, because I'll be waiting for you to call me and it doesn't matter if it's even in the middle of the night."

"Tristan." I cut him off, seriously we'll be here all day.

"Okay, okay." He hugs everyone a second time.

"Thanks so much." I hug my mom and then my dad. "We really appreciate this."

"You kids have fun."

"We will." Tristan smiles as he shakes my father's hand, "Thank you. Call me anytime because...."

"Tristan," everyone yells, cutting him off.

He holds his hands up in surrender. "Okay, okay. Get in the car, woman." He tries to act tough as he opens my car door for me.

"Bye everyone," I call. "I'm so excited."

Tristan closes the door, gets behind the wheel and looks over at me. "Are you ready for your babymoon, Mrs. Miles?"

I smirk. "You bet your fucking life I am."

———

The plane touches down on the runway and I smile over at my traveling partner.

We are heading to Jameson's luxury beach house in Miami, it was as beachy as we could get without leaving the US. With me being this pregnant, Tristan was too nervous to leave the country.

I peer out the window of the private jet to see the car on the tarmac waiting for us, I just can't wait to get there.

Three days later.

I lie on the deckchair and smile up at the sun, topless and pregnant and good lord I must look a treat. The sun on my skin is too perfect to cover up.

Tristan is sleeping on his deckchair beside me and this is the most relaxed I have ever seen him. He's been so busy with work and the kids and the house and preparing for the baby, he literally hasn't stopped for months.

We needed this.

Time away on our own to breathe. To take the time to enjoy each other, no thinking about dinner, no chores and no kids squabbling over the dinner table.

Just the two of us and all the loud sex we can have.

And trust me, we've had a lot. I think the paint is peeling off the walls from the things it has seen.

We had cheese and biscuits for dinner last night, and it was fucking perfect.

We lay by the pool and watched the sun go down, Tris drank cocktails, I drank mocktails and we ate our weight in cheese and biscuits. By the time it came around for us to go out to dinner we were both full and didn't feel like going. So we had a two-hour soak in the hot tub instead.

I pick up Tristan's notepad and pen and read through the names we have narrowed it down to. Is there anything harder than choosing a baby's name?

TOP CHOICES.

GIRLS

- **Summer**

- Phoebe
- Sage
- Micha
- Arna
- Poppy
- Violet
- Keeley

BOYS

- William—Billy
- Evan
- Arlo
- Regan
- Art
- Nate
- Braxton
- Cooper

I smile as I go over the names, Tris has put so much thought into this.

"What are you thinking?" he asks, his voice still sleepy.

I glance over. "I don't know." I twist my lips as I go over the list. "I want a name that goes with the other boys' names but then it has to sound strong with Miles."

"Anderson-Miles," he replies.

I glance over to him. "What do you mean?"

"I want the baby's surname to be Anderson-Miles, I want it to have the same surname as its mother and brothers."

"You want the baby to have Wade's surname?"

He shrugs. "He's sharing his sons with me, it's only fair I share my child with him. He's a part of this family too."

My eyes well with tears as I stare at him.

Just when you think you couldn't love someone more than you already do.

"No, Tristan. You will not share this baby with anyone. You are its father and its surname will be Miles and only Miles."

He gives me the best come-fuck-me look of all time.

I sit up and lean over and kiss him softly. "You have no idea how much it means to me that you offered that." My lips linger over his. "My god, I love you so much," I whisper. "How do I ever deserve you?"

He cups my face in his hands as our kiss deepens. "You should probably suck my dick to prove it."

I giggle, typical Tristan Miles answer, nothing will ever change. "It always comes back to sucking dick with you, doesn't it?"

He smiles and pulls me down on top of him, "You know it, wench. Get busy."

———

Tristan sways me to the music on the dance floor. "I don't want to go home tomorrow." He smiles against my temple.

"Me neither." I smile against his lips. "Thank you, this has been one of the best weeks of my life."

And it has, swimming, sunning, laughing and love.

So much love.

"It has." He smiles wistfully as he looks out over the crowd. "I'm nervous about the baby coming."

"You are?" I frown. "Why, you are a natural with kids?"

"It means less time with you."

My eyes search his. "You will never have less time with me."

"We both know that's not true. Our time together is already so...."

"Crowded?" I smile.

He smirks as if not wanting to elaborate.

"Tris." I look up at him. "One day, these children will all be gone, moved out and living their own lives and it will be just me and you. All alone in our big old house."

"Promise?"

My heart breaks a little, this is the first time in our relationship that he has ever admitted that he needs more alone time. I need to make more of an effort after the baby comes. "I promise." We keep swaying to the music. "We should make a new family tradition."

"What's that?"

"You and I should come back here every year on our own for a week. Just the two of us."

He smiles down at me. "We could do that."

"Maybe next year we can make another baby or maybe even twins."

He winces. "Calm down, Anderson. Fuck."

I giggle and he takes my lips in his with a perfect kiss, tender and loving. Hot and heavy, all the things that my beautiful husband is. His hand slides over my pregnant stomach as he holds me close, I feel his arousal roll in like a fog. We are so physically in sync, it's like we share a body. "I need to get you home, Mrs. Miles."

I smile up at him. "Well that depends."

"On what?"

"On whether you are going to do bad things to my body."

"That can be arranged." He smiles darkly as he runs his

hand over my stomach once more. "Well, as bad as I can do with you in this condition."

"You mean the beach ball condition?"

He pulls me by the hand off the dance floor. "I'm talking the orca whale condition."

I burst out laughing and so does he. "Are you calling me a whale?" I fake gasp.

"Don't worry, I love whales." He picks up my coat and handbag. "Especially fucking them."

I laugh out loud. "You need to stop talking now, Mr. Miles."

"I know."

I lie on my side in the darkness, the room is lit only by a lamp and Tristan is lying behind me, his body butted up close to mine. He has my top leg hooked over his forearm as his hand rests protectively over my stomach.

His thick cock slides into my wet flesh and I whimper as my body ripples around his, this is our position of choice right now. We can kiss, and he can fuck me deep without fear of hurting me.

Not that he ever could.

His grip on my stomach gets tighter as he gets faster, the bed begins to hit the wall and I moan, deep and low.

So. Fucking. Good.

"Fuck me," I whimper into his mouth. "Fuck me deep."

His eyes flicker with arousal as he picks up the pace, his hips moving at piston pace. The sound of my wet body sucking him in echoes around the room. He reaches up and pinches my nipple and I convulse into an orgasm; I cry out as he does too.

He holds himself deep and I feel the jerk of his cock as it empties inside of me.

He grabs my face and kisses me so tenderly that I melt into him.

We are so in love.

Tristan

Tomorrow is the day.

"Okay, so we have nightgowns." Patrick and I are doing a last check on Claire's hospital bag. I was looking in Claire's purse for something today and I found a list from the hospital about what she should bring with her, it's the first time I've seen it. She is completely disregarding the list.

Patrick and I are not.

I fold the four nightgowns and put them on a pile on the bed, I've checked this bag ten times but I keep getting the feeling that we have forgotten something. Now that I have a list I can finally check it for real.

Claire is way too relaxed about all of this, she could care less about what we could forget. It's a disaster waiting to happen.

"What else is on the list, Tricky?" I ask.

"Toilet rees bag." Patrick sounds it out.

I put the toiletries bag on the bed. "Check."

"Sanitary...."

"Check." I put the three packets of pads onto the bed.

Patrick picks up a packet and turns it around to look at the back. "What even are these things?"

"Pillows for the baby." I snatch the packet off him and put it onto the bed.

"Black underpants." He continues reading, he looks up at me. "Why do they have to be black?"

"I don't know, weird girls' stuff." I shrug. "Who knows what goes on down there. Next?"

"Socks."

I throw six pairs of socks onto the bed. "Actually, she probably needs more." I go to her drawer and get another two pairs out.

"Clothes for the baby."

"What?" I frown.

"It says here...clothes for the baby."

"Give me that." I snatch the list from him. "She never told me that we needed to pack clothes for the baby."

He shrugs. "I don't know."

I catch sight of Claire outside in the hall. "Claire," I call. "Come here please."

She walks in. "Yeah?"

"Did you forget something?" I widen my eyes at her. "Something very important."

"Like what?"

"Like clothes for the baby?" I gasp. "Do you think this child is going to be a nudist? Like what, is it going to just freeball in the hospital chucking leg-spreads everywhere?"

"You idiot?" She rolls her eyes. "So.... Go pack clothes for the baby, then." She saunters back out of the room without a care in the world.

"Fucking unbelievable," I mutter under my breath. "Now I'm going to need a whole new bag."

"What for?"

"Clothes for the baby, Patrick. What bag will we use?"

Patrick thinks for a moment and shrugs.

I march out into the hallway and call down the stairs. "Claire, what bag will I pack clothes for the baby in?"

Silence....

"Claire?"

"The nappy bag, Tristan," she replies deadpan.

"Ahh...." I nod. "But don't we need that for the nappies?"

"You're killing me," she calls back.

I'll fucking kill you in a minute.

I march back to the bedroom. "Your mother said use the nappy bag."

"But isn't that for nappies?" Patrick frowns.

"That's exactly what I said." I walk into the baby's room and look around for Patrick. "Well, are you coming?"

"Yes." Patrick sighs as he saunters in and sits on the rocking chair in the corner of the room.

"Oh, am I inconveniencing you?" I huff.

He lies back and kicks his legs up over the arm of the chair.

"I'll have you know, Patrick, that you have a baby brother or sister arriving tomorrow and it is our job to make sure it has clothes to wear."

He looks at me deadpan.

"Because your mother obviously doesn't care."

"I heard that," Claire calls from our bedroom.

"Stop eavesdropping on our conversations," I call back.

"Okay." I open the wardrobe doors; sweet little baby clothes are all hanging up on tiny, cute hangers, and a rush of excitement runs through me.

Tomorrow.

"Okay." I open a drawer. "What should we pack?" I pull out a singlet, it's teeny tiny and about thirty centimeters long, I glance back over my shoulder to Patrick. "Does your mother think we are having a snake?"

He shrugs. "I don't know."

"You don't know much, do you?"

He shrugs again.

I grab a pile of snake singlets and put them onto the change table. "Nappies."

I tap my temple. "Aha, for the nappy bag." I grab a pile of nappies and put them on the change table.

"Going-out clothes," Patrick says.

"Hmm." I look around the wardrobe. "What does a baby class as going-out clothes?"

Patrick shrugs. "I don't know."

Fuck's sake.

I march back into my bedroom to see Claire lying on the bed with her eyes closed, she looks so peaceful but we have shit to do, there is absolutely no time for sleeping. "Claire." I tap her on the foot. "Claire."

"What, Tristan?" She sighs as if I am the biggest inconvenience in the world.

This is inconvenient to me too, you know?

"How many outfits should I pack for the baby?"

She opens one eye to look at me. "What do you mean, outfits?"

"Outfits, clothes." I widen my eyes; how does she not know what that means?

"The baby doesn't wear outfits, Tris."

"What do you mean?"

"It will wear onesies."

"What?" I screw up my face. "All the time?"

"They are comfortable." She closes her eyes again. "I was just going to throw a bag together tonight, don't stress about it. If I need anything while we are at the hospital you can just bring it up."

"Oh." I stare at her for a moment, I feel so dumb at all of this.

She taps the bed beside her. "Right now I need a hug from my husband."

I lie down beside her and she takes me into her arms and kisses my forehead. "You're very cute packing the bags. Thank you."

I roll my eyes.

Cute.

"You're going to be the best dad." She smiles with her eyes closed. "This baby is so lucky." She runs her fingers through my hair as I mentally go through what else I need to do today.

"Are you having an affair with a snake?" I ask.

"What?" Her eyes open in surprise.

"The singlets you bought are not human, they're for a baby snake."

She bursts out laughing. "They are long so you can tuck them in, you idiot."

"Oh." I smirk. "That makes more sense."

"What are you doing?" Patrick calls. "Muffy, no."

"What's happening in there?" I yell.

"Muff is sitting in the nappy bag."

I fly out of bed like a maniac. "If that cat pisses in the nappy bag it is genuinely meeting its maker."

———

I change into the robe and put the hairnet on. I put the medical booties on over my shoes and wash my hands.

I'm sick with nerves.

Claire is being prepped for surgery. Because she has had what they call three unsuccessful natural births in the past she is having a scheduled C-section.

"Are you ready, Mr. Miles?" the nurse asks me.

"Yes."

Thump.

Thump.

Thump goes my heart.

"This way, please."

I follow the nurse into the operating theater and see Claire all gowned up with a hairnet on. She smiles over at me. "Hey you."

"Hi." I feel faint.

A screen is up between her and her stomach, the sound of two heartbeats echoes through the room and my heart twists. A huge light hangs above the operating table.

This is full on.

"You can sit here." The nurse pulls me up a chair beside the bed and I sit down and take Claire's hand in mine. "Oh my god, are you okay?" I whisper as I kiss her forehead. "Are you okay?"

She smiles and nods. "It's fine, babe, calm down. It's going to be fine."

Such a Claire thing to say, always worrying about everyone else but herself.

"Hello, Tristan. Let's deliver your baby, shall we?" the doctor says casually as if he does this every day.

I mean, he probably does but whatever.

"Sounds good." I keep my eyes focused on Claire and in my peripheral vision I can see the doctor and nurses moving. Claire's body jiggles around a little and I screw up my face and kiss her temple. "I love you," I whisper.

Her body moves around some more as if they are moving her and she has no control and I feel like I can't breathe.

My god.

I cling to Claire's hand so tightly, please be okay.

Please be okay.

If something were to happen to her....

Her body moves quite violently and she closes her eyes as if in pain.

"Did that hurt?" I stammer.

"No. Just a weird sensation." She smiles up at me. "I'm okay."

I nod nervously and my eyes flick over to the doctors, what's taking so long?

Her body moves again and the curtain is dropped in time to see them lift the baby out of her stomach. It's covered in white stuff and chubby and big. It cries out loud and Claire laughs. "It's a little girl." The doctor smiles.

A girl.

My eyes widen.

A girl.

They lift the baby to lie on Claire's chest and Claire kisses her forehead. "Happy birthday, sweetheart," she whispers.

Their silhouette blurs.

"Tristan," Claire whispers though tears. "Look at her."

I kiss the baby's tiny head and then Claire's as I hold them tight.

The tears won't stop and I wipe my eyes with the back of my hands. "I love you. So much." I hold Claire close as we both stare at the perfect little girl. "I love you too, baby."

The nurse comes over. "We need to check the baby's vitals over now."

She goes to take the baby and Claire's eyes flick to me. "Go with her."

"What?"

"You stay with the baby, do not take your eyes off her for a second."

"What about you?" My eyes flick to the doctor.

"We will be stitching here for a while; Claire will meet the two of you back at the room," the doctor says.

What?

I want us all to stay together, I don't want to leave Claire here alone.

No.

The nurse wraps the baby and Claire's eyes flick to me once more. "Go with her, Tristan, don't leave her alone."

My eyes flick between Claire and the baby....

"She needs you," Claire whispers.

Hearing those words wakes something up in me, something I've never experienced before.

"Okay." On autopilot, I stand, and with my heart in my throat I follow the nurse out of the operating theater. I glance back to my love lying alone on the operating table and for the first time in my life I get it.

Being a parent is putting your baby before yourself... every time in every circumstance.

We walk through to another room and I watch on silently as the baby is weighed, her little wristband is put on. They do a heel-prick test and she screams loudly.

"She didn't like that, listen to those strong lungs." The nurse laughs.

I smile through tears, she's feisty like her mom.

The nurse wipes her face and dresses her and then wraps her up tightly in a pink bunny blanket, she puts her into a crib on wheels. "Let's take you to the room."

I follow the nurse down the corridor as I have some kind of out-of-body moment.

Everything is so casual, as if this is just any normal day.

But it's not just any day.

A perfect little soul has just entered the world, it's monumental.

We get to Claire's room and I look around, it's not right that she isn't here yet. That the boys aren't here yet.

"You can hold her while you wait for Claire."

I stare at her wide eyed, I don't know if I'm in shock or what?

"Sit in the chair and I'll pass her to you."

"Okay." I fall into the recliner in the corner and the nurse picks up the baby and passes her to me.

Oh....

I stare at her perfect little face as she stares up at me.

"Hi," I whisper. "You're so pretty."

She has dark hair like me, long eyelashes, and rosy lips. So perfect.

I run my finger down her face and try and memorize this moment in time. Take every single second on the record because I know that as long as I live that I never want to forget this feeling.

She reaches up and grabs my finger, my heart stops, and my eyes well with tears anew. This is a real living little person, with her own heart and mind.

A piece of me and Claire.

Oh my god.

I hear clattering coming down the corridor outside and I hear Claire's laugh.

She's here.

I stand and with our bundled-up tiny baby in my arms I wait for my wife. Claire comes into view and the tears start again.

My god, stop it.

Claire laughs when she sees me. "Here they are. My two babies."

They wheel Claire in and check all of her vitals as we both stand in the corner and wait patiently. She's hooked up to blood-pressure machines.

"Do you want to hold her?" I ask.

She nods and I carefully pass her over, she's so small that I'm scared I'm going to break her.

"Hey, bubba." She smiles as she looks down at her. "You are so cute."

I get a lump in my throat as I watch on.

She rearranges her and the nurse lifts her onto her nipple and she begins to suck.

How the hell does she know how to do that already?

My kid is a genius.

The nurses finally leave us alone and I sit on the side of the bed and kiss Claire's forehead.

There are no words for what I'm feeling.

Love drunk....

"Tris." Claire smiles down at her. "She's perfect."

"Like you." I hold her close. "Thank you, I have never loved you more."

We both smile down at her.

"What do you want to name her?" Claire asks. "It's your pick, I like all of the names on your list so it's up to you."

I stare down at her and smile, I know exactly what to call her. "Summer Claire Miles."

Claire's eyes cloud over. "It's the perfect name."

"For the perfect child, did you see how smart she is knowing how to do that when she was born like five minutes ago?"

Claire giggles.

"The kid is a genius."

"Patrick, walk faster." We hear squabbling from the corridor. The boys come into view and they all stop at the door, wide eyed.

"Come and meet your sister, boys." I smile proudly.

"A girl?" Patrick frowns.

Claire smiles. "A little girl."

Harry winces. "A girl?"

"Yes, a girl," I snap.

Thank fuck not another boy.

The boys all crowd around the bed and watch on in silence, half shocked. Who am I kidding, completely shocked.

As am I.

"Her name is Summer." Claire smiles dreamily as she looks down at her. "Summer Miles."

The boys all goo and ga over her.

She finishes feeding and Claire rewraps her.

Harry holds his arms out. "Can I hold her?"

I break into a cold sweat; I get an image of him accidently dropping her on her head or some shit. "Um...." I glance to Claire.

"Let her rest now, baby, she's had a big day, you can hold her tonight."

Phew....

I stand back and look around the room at my four children and wife.

So much to love.

Claire

I watch Summer sleep in her crib, so peaceful and serene. Her little arms are up by her face and every now and then she sucks her bottom lip. She has dark hair and olive skin, rosy lips.

An angel.

She looks so much like her dad; the perfect little bundle of joy and I had no idea the level of peace she would bring me. It's as if my whole being has let out a deep sigh of relief.

She's here.

A little girl to love forever. I was a young mother last time, caught in a whirlwind of business. Desperate to keep working and prove my worth to myself and the world.

This time will be different, nothing else matters. I know my worth now and I'm going to savor every single second of time with this beloved baby girl.

"Knock, knock," sounds at the door.

"Come in."

"Hello, is now a good time?"

A familiar face comes into view with a huge bunch of flowers and I laugh. "Gabriel, you came to visit me."

"Ahhh, bella." He kisses my cheeks and holds my arms as he looks me over. "Look at you, all glowing and momlike." He glances over to the crib. "This is her."

"It is," I gush. "Look how beautiful she is."

This is a big deal for Gabriel to come here and see me, he and Tristan don't get along and although I know that will never change, they do tolerate each other for me.

He smiles down at the crib and rubs his hand over her hair. "So precious."

"She is, isn't she?"

"What is her name?"

"Summer."

He smiles.

"Summer Miles." He raises an eyebrow and I giggle. "Don't say it."

"Her complexion is so dark compared to your other children," he says as he looks her over.

"She looks just like her father."

"Oh." He softly strokes her hair with his fingertips. "You poor darling."

I go to sit up and wince and he frowns. "What's happening, are you in pain?"

"I had a C-section."

He frowns. "Why?"

"Long story, it was planned, I'll be fine in a few days."

"I bought you flowers." He digs something out of his pocket and passes over a little pink gift box. "Open it later."

"Don't you want to see what Gracie bought us?" I smirk.

He chuckles. "You know me too well, Claire." He takes a seat on the chair in the corner of the room.

"How *is* Gracie?" I ask.

"She's leaving me."

"What?" I frown. "What do you mean?"

"She's bought a place in god knows where and has handed in her resignation. Her last day is on Friday."

My face falls. "Well...did you tell her?"

"Tell her what?"

"That you're hopelessly in love with her."

He rolls his eyes. "Where do you come up with this shit? I am not in love with Gracie."

"Yes, you are."

"Why the fuck would you say that?"

"Because it's true."

He exhales heavily. "You have no idea what you're talking about."

"Yes. I do, I've seen the way you look at her. You've loved her for years."

"Enough."

"Well...you need to stop her from leaving."

"I already tried. She won't stay." He puffs air into his cheeks. "It's probably for the best anyway."

I watch him for a moment, I know him, he would be really down about this.

"Anyway." He sits up. "I just popped in for a quick visit, I have to go before the firing squad arrives."

I giggle.

"Can you take a photo of me holding Summer to put on the front page of *Ferrara News* tomorrow?" He winks.

"Can you imagine?"

"Maybe I could be her godfather." He raises his eyebrow mischievously.

"Tristan would have a heart attack."

"That's the point of it."

"You are so bad." I giggle. "Behave."

The way Gabriel purposely baits the Miles brothers is next level. If we hadn't been such good friends before I met

Tristan, I wouldn't understand it. But Gabriel's different, he isn't who they see.

I know the real him.

Mind you, I don't blame them at all for disliking him. Tristan and I have had the biggest fights in our relationship over my friendship with Gabe, but he's staying in my life. It's nonnegotiable, he was a dear, dear friend to me after Wade died and at a time when I felt totally alone, he always had my back.

As much as Tristan dislikes him, I know he respects him because of how he's protected me in the past. Not that he'll ever admit it.

He stands and takes my hand in his. "Congratulations, bella, you deserve to be happy."

I smile up at him as I hold his hand in mine. "So do you."

He exhales heavily. "Maybe one day."

"You hate that you like Gracie that way, don't you?"

"I hate meddling friends more." He kisses my cheek. "Call me when you can have lunch."

"Thank you for coming, it means a lot."

He disappears out the door and I turn back to my full-time position of Summer staring.

Sigh.... *She's so perfect.*

———

"Here we are. Home sweet home." Tristan smiles as he pulls into the driveway.

The boys are all lined up on the veranda waiting with a bunch of flowers each, I giggle. "How long have they been waiting there?"

Tristan throws me a sexy wink and comes around and

helps me out of the car, the boys come rushing out and clamber around us.

"Thank god you're finally home," Patrick moans. "It's been so long."

Tristan goes to the back seat and unlatches Summer's little carrier; he carefully carries her inside to hushed excitement of the boys.

Fletcher opens the door and Tristan carefully walks into the house with Summer, he stumbles and trips on a football boot, he goes careering toward a wall and just stops himself in time.

"Shoes in the foyer," he hisses through gritted teeth as he looks around to the boys.

"Sorry," Patrick whispers, he picks up the boots and opens the door and hurls them out the front door.

"Quite sure they don't go there either." Tristan widens his eyes.

"I'll get them later," Patrick replies. "Can I hold her now?"

"Let's show Summer her bedroom first." I smile.

To the excited whispers of the boys, Tristan carries the carrier upstairs and down to her bedroom. "So help me god," he whispers angrily. "I'm going to kill that fucking cat."

"Don't swear in front of her," Patrick cries.

We've been drilling into the boys about using appropriate language in front of the baby.

"What are you talking about?" I look around the room and then I see it and burst out laughing.

Muff the cat is curled up asleep in Summer's cot.

Tristan passes me the carrier. "Hold this, darling," he says a little too sweetly.

"Don't...."

He picks Muff up and pretends to whisper in her ear. "You

are going to meet a grisly end, my friend. Mark my words." He puts her outside the room and closes the door. "Where were we?" He looks around the room at the boys all gathered around Summer on the floor.

"I believe we were in heaven," I say as I watch the four of them together.

He smiles and kisses me softly. "I know we are."

———

I look at the empty cradle and roll my eyes. "Where is my baby?" Not in her cradle as usual, I walk downstairs to find Tristan lying on the couch with Summer bundled up and sleeping in his arms. He cannot leave her alone, he wants to hold her all the time. Between him and the boys she is never left alone for even a second.

They are obsessed.

"What are you doing?" I ask him.

"Watching television, what does it look like?"

"Why is Summer not in her crib?"

"She was lonely."

"She was asleep, Tristan. You don't get lonely when you are asleep."

"She's so little, she hates being up there by herself. She said she likes to be down here with me."

"She said that?" I look at him deadpan.

"Uh-huh."

"She's ten days old, she can't speak."

"Telepathically, Claire, telepathically." He taps his temple and then looks down at his daughter. "You like sleeping on me, don't you, baby? I'm the ultimate mattress."

I smirk because they really are so cute together. "This is

all great for when you are home, Tris, but you are creating a monster here. When you go back to work, I can't sit still all day while she sleeps in my arms, I have a household to run. You are only making it harder for her."

He looks up at me unimpressed.

"She needs to go back to her crib."

"Maybe you should go back to work, then, and I'll stay home," he mumbles as he kisses her tiny head. "You can sleep on me all day long," he says in a baby voice.

I point to the stairs. "Crib."

"Five more minutes." He turns back to the television.

"I'm going to the shops quickly with Mom to pick up some things, are you okay to watch her for half an hour?"

"Uh-huh," He smiles as if glad that I'm leaving.

I smile back. "You're not going to put her back in her crib, are you?"

"Not a chance."

Five years later.

"I'm going, Mom," Fletcher calls.

"Hang on, I'm coming."

I swaddle Billy up in his blanket and make my way downstairs, Fletcher is going back to his place after staying here last night.

He lives in Tristan's penthouse in Tribeca now, all grown up and not my little baby anymore. He's got new friends that are more suited to him and the stage of life he is in. Some of them are stockbrokers, a doctor, a law student.... All playboys I bet, not that I want to know anything about that.

We have six children now, our three older boys and then

we had two little girls, Summer and Poppy, and then another little boy, William, who we call Billy.

We walk Fletcher out the front, Tristan has a daughter on each hip and Patrick takes Billy from me and holds him.

Harry is staying with Elliot and Kate, he's doing work experience in the London office, he's been with them for six weeks now and seems to be having the time of his life. He's doing an internship with Miles Media just like Fletcher did at his age and loving every second of it...I'm not quite sure Jameson knew what he was getting himself into there.

Fletcher throws his basket of washing into the passenger seat of his Porsche. "You know you have a washing machine at your place, right?" Tristan mutters dryly.

"Yeah."

I giggle. "He doesn't know how to use it."

Tristan walks around the car inspecting it. "You need to wash your car."

"I know, Dad." He rolls his eyes.

"I still can't believe you bought a Porsche." I sigh as I look it over, I hardly recognize my little boy anymore. Power suit, power car, penthouse, and player friends.

A Miles man through and through.

"He worked hard for it," Tristan scoffs. "What's the point of waiting until you are sixty to buy the car of your dreams? Life is short, Claire; you've got to play hard."

Fletcher kisses us all and hugs me extra tight.

"I hate it when you leave."

"He'll be back tomorrow." Tristan rolls his eyes.

Tristan doesn't miss him as much as I do because he sees him every day at work.

Anderson Media is booming and they are busier than ever.

Fletcher gets into the car and we watch it disappear down the road as we wave.

Life is different now, quieter but louder. Busier but calmer. Grown up but then still just babies.

It's like my life has had two parts. The life before Tristan and the life we live now.

"Can I go to a party tonight?" Patrick asks.

"No," Tristan replies as we walk back inside. "You're grounded, remember?"

I smirk, our sweet little Tricky has turned into quite the ratbag, got caught drinking last weekend. Him and his friends drank a cask of wine in the garage and they would have got away with it too if Patrick didn't come staggering out blind drunk.

"Can my friends come over?"

"No."

"What am I supposed to do all weekend, then?" Patrick moans as we walk up the front steps.

Tristan glares at him. "Try not to get murdered."

THE CASANOVA EPILOGUE

THE MILES HIGH CLUB

* Trigger warning - The sensitive issue of fertility is discussed in this epilogue.

1

THE CASANOVA EPILOGUE

Kate

THE PRIVATE JET touches down and I hunch my shoulders up in excitement as I look over at my new husband. "Where are we?"

He winks and taps the side of his nose.

"You are *still* not telling me where we are going for our honeymoon?"

"Not yet."

"Well at least tell me what country are we in?"

"Nope."

"Elliot." I laugh. "Come on, this is ridiculous."

He leans over, takes my face in his hands, and kisses me softly. "It's called a surprise, Kate." His lips linger over mine.

"I love it already." I smile.

"You do?"

"Uh-huh and I love you."

He smiles against my lips. "I love you too."

The plane taxis to its eventual resting place and I sit back and smile, so much has happened. So many magical memories have been made.

I got married to my dream man, on a dreamy farm, and now he has some colossal surprise for me and I have no idea what it is.

Only that he's really excited about it, which means it must be special because Elliot only gets excited about super-special romantic things.

We climb off, I'm instantly hit with cool air and I frown as I look around. "Where is this place?"

Elliot smiles and gestures to the black car that is waiting on the tarmac. "Into the car, my love. We have a long drive ahead of us."

"We do?" I frown as I look around. *Where the actual fuck are we?*

For some reason I just assumed we would go somewhere hot and tropical.

"Are we in Japan?" I ask.

"I don't know, are we?"

"Elliot," I laugh. "Come on, tell me."

"You'll find out soon enough, into the car, Miss Impatience."

"It's Mrs. Miles, actually."

He gives me the best come-fuck-me look of all time. "That's right, it is." He kisses me, a little tongue, and a whole lot of naughty promise. "Mrs. Miles has a ring to it, doesn't it?"

I hold up my hand and show him my wedding ring. "Sure does."

He chuckles and opens the car door for me and I scoot on in.

. . .

The car comes to a halt and I peer out the window.

What the heck is this place?

Elliot gets out and opens my door and helps me out of the car, I look around in question. "Where are we?"

Elliot's eyes glow with affection. "I thought that seeing your parents couldn't come to our wedding, they should choose our honeymoon."

I frown.

"We're at the Inca Trail."

My eyes widen and I look around. "This is...you mean?"

He nods.

Tears instantly well in my eyes, doing this trek was my parents' biggest goal in life. It was their bucket list trip, the one they never got to take. "Oh Elliot," I cry.

"Stop with the blubbering," sounds from behind me, I turn in a rush to see Brad, my brother, and my face falls again.

"I thought Brad should be here to do this with you," Elliot says softly. "With us."

My heart free-falls from my chest.

Just when you think you couldn't love someone any more than you do.

I screw up my face in tears, Elliot is sharing his honeymoon with my brother so that we can take our parents' dream trip together.

My heart swells in my chest, this is the most beautiful, thoughtful gift of love that anyone could ever give me.

Of course Elliot did this, it's so him.

"I love you so much." I jump into Elliot's arms. "You are the most romantic man of all time." I kiss him. "I love you." I kiss him again. "I love you. I love you."

Elliot and Brad chuckle at my over-the-top reaction.

"Don't be fooled," Brad replies. "He brought me so I could carry his ass up the hill."

I laugh through tears. "Probably."

Elliot

The morning sun filters through the kitchen, flickering beams of gold splay generously across the timber parquetry floors. It's chilly this morning and I rub my hands together as I wait for my coffee to pour.

I look through the window down to the sandstone building at the bottom of the hill, Kate wasn't in bed when I woke this morning and I know exactly where she is. We converted one of the old buildings on the property into the perfect art studio.

Kate's happy place.

I make my two cups of coffee, put my gum boots on and head off in search of my girl.

I trudge down the hill and pass our goats on the top paddock, we have a family of four now. Gretel and Billy have been busy and blissfully quiet, it seems regular sex will keep even the naughtiest of goats well behaved. He's a new man...goat.

I keep walking down hill, it's so cold that when I breathe, puffs of fog fill the air. I put the cups down on the steps and roll open the huge heavy door and smile, I stand for a moment and watch her; she's working on a huge painting and my god...is it beautiful.

Kate is my favorite thing on earth and her paintings are my second favorite, the fact that one makes the other is simply incredible.

She catches me from the corner of her eye. "Hey." She smiles.

"Good morning. Missed you this morning."

She walks over and kisses me. "I didn't want to wake you."

I pass over her cup of coffee and smile up at the painting in awe. "I thought Sunday was a rest day."

"It is, but this isn't work, is it?"

"My god, Kate. It's perfection." I sigh dreamily.

She flicks her unruly hair out of the way. "You like it?"

"I love it." My eyes roam over the huge abstract, she's been working on it for weeks and every time I see it, it gets better.

"I love you." She smiles. "I've been thinking."

I sip my coffee. "About what?"

"I think I want to go off the pill."

I frown. "What?"

She shrugs. "I think it's time."

My eyebrows rise in surprise.

"What do you think?"

"That's the furthest thing from my mind."

Her face falls. "Oh."

Sensing her disappointment, I put my coffee down and take her into my arms. "I just found you, call me selfish, but I want you to myself for a while."

"You didn't just find me." She smiles. "We've been married for eighteen months, El."

"And what a perfect eighteen months it has been, it isn't that long, is it?"

"It is."

"Feels like a minute." I exhale heavily, I knew this

conversation would come one day and to be honest, I've been dreading it. "Don't you like our life as it is?"

"I do."

"So why change it?"

"I know you want children."

"Maybe not." I shrug. "Who knows what the future brings?"

She frowns and pulls out of my arms. "What?"

"I don't know, I feel complete. I want for nothing; my life is perfect how it is. We travel whenever we want, we do whatever we want. We have no ties and I love the freedom of it being just us."

She stares up at me.

"You won't be able to just pop down here and paint for ten hours, having a baby would change ours and especially *your* entire life, and you need to really think about this."

She nods. "You're right."

I kiss her softly. "I don't need to have children. It's not a must-have bucket list thing for me."

She stares up at me as she listens, this is the first time I've been honest with her on this subject.

"My life feels complete, the day I married you everything clicked into place and I got a sense of finality."

Her face falls. "You don't think we are going to have children, do you?"

My heart sinks, I don't.

"I'm not sure," I whisper softly.

"What brought this on, is this your gut instincts telling you this?"

I stay silent.

She stares at me and then frowns. "You think that we

won't be able to have a baby and have made peace with it already, haven't you?"

I stare at her, that's exactly what I've done.

"Sweetheart, isn't our family of two enough?" I ask.

She twists her lips, seemingly annoyed.

"We don't need children to be happy, we're already happy."

"I know."

"And just because having a baby is the normal for everyone else, it doesn't mean that we have to do it." I brush the hair back from her forehead as I look down at her. "Life is perfect as it is."

She nods and stares into space, and I know I've lost her. Her mind is off on a tangent.

Or maybe she's just pissed....

"We go to Paris tomorrow," I remind her.

She smiles and nods. "Yep."

"Why don't you come up to the house and I'll make us some breakfast."

"I'm not really hungry." She kisses me softly. "I'll be up later."

"Okay."

She goes back to painting and I stand at the door and watch her with a heavy heart.

I want her to have everything in life that she's ever wanted, but for some reason and I don't even know why, my gut tells me this is the one thing we won't get.

I can't watch her suffer throughout the process; it will kill me.

I make my way up to the house; I'm going to make her breakfast anyway.

It's a chocolate pancake kind of day.

Kate

Paris.

"You nearly ready to go, babe?" Elliot calls.

"Just a minute." I call. I turn and look at my behind and then turn back to the front and stare at my reflection. Who is that girl in the mirror?

My hair is out and full and I'm wearing red lipstick.

My outfit consists of a black tight pencil skirt, black cashmere fitted top, patent leather sky high pumps and my gold Rolex watch.

Dressed in Chanel from head to toe, I'm hardly recognizable.

It's weird, you know. When I first started dating Elliot I never thought I would dress this way, or ever own a fancy handbag. I thought that everything he owned was stupidly overpriced and wanky, don't get me wrong, it still is. But little by little you get used to having money, to owning ridiculously expensive designer things. Elliot said something one day when we first met whilst shopping and it stayed with me.

If you give the paparazzi something to talk about, be it your clothes or your shoes or your watch ...then they don't talk about you.

And he was right, they've left me alone.

Elliot comes around the door, his eyes drop to my toes and back up to my face, he gives me a slow sexy smile and does a low whistle.

"Fuck, my wife is hot." He steps forward, takes me into his arms and kisses me, his tongue brushing against mine. "Are you ready to go and sell some paintings Harriet Boucher?"

He squeezes my behind in his hands as his lips drop to my neck.

I stretch my neck to give him better access and smile as his teeth graze my skin, "I am."

We decided to keep the pseudonym Harriet Boucher, although we have let out my true name.

Elanor went to prison for eight months for fraud. She was forced to pay back the money she stole, although only half of it was ever recovered because she'd spent the rest of it. She's going out with some famous Formula One driver now and seems happy enough.

I call her on her birthday and Christmas. She doesn't call me ever. One day I will completely let go of the dream of trying to salvage our relationship. But for now, she's still my sister who has just lost her way. I'm hoping she returns to the Elanor I once loved.

Elliot hates her with a passion, there is no chance ever of a reconciliation between the two of them.

"Come on."

I grab my purse and he takes my hand in his, "Let's go."

Elliot

The crowd hushes as Kate walks through the art gallery, she eclipses everyone in the room.

I'm used to people staring at my brothers and I, but Kate.... she's an enigma. She doesn't have any idea just how talented she is.

But they do, and so do I.

I'm just the lucky prick that she happened to fall in love with.

"Auction number fifteen." The auctioneer calls. "We have a Harriet Boucher painted by Katherine Miles."

The room falls silent and I smile proudly as adrenaline surges through my system, I will never get enough of this.

Seeing her heart come through in the paintings, watching them fall in love with her through paint splayed on a canvas.

Knowing that she was calling to me all along.

It's here, in the art galleries, where I see her paintings hanging on the wall, being admired by all, that I count my blessings a million times over.

For not so long ago, I would stare at her paintings for hours and wish for her to come true.

And she did.

In beautiful technicolor.

"This is the most precious work we have seen tonight." The auctioneer calls.

Kate smiles bashfully and fuck, my heart somersaults in my chest.

"Can we start the bidding at three hundred thousand?"

I look over to my private bidder and rub my nose, our secret code for yes.

He holds up his card.

"Three hundred thousand."

It doesn't matter that I married Kate Landon or Harriet Boucher or that she's my wife Kate Miles, nothing has changed. I have to have all of her paintings, every single one of them and damn it, nothing can stop me.

Not even her.

She won't let me bid, tells me that I can have them for free, so I secretly hire someone to do it for me. While ever the prices are still going up at auction, it only makes her collection more valuable.

"Six hundred."

"Seven twenty."

"Nine hundred."

Kate bites her bottom lip to keep herself from smiling.

I run my hand through my hair. "One point one." My bidder calls.

"One point four." A woman calls.

I smile at the ground, I love that this woman loves it, I bid against her at every auction. It's almost tempting to let her have it.

Almost....

I rub my nose again, "One point six." My bidder calls.

The room hushes as they wait for the next bid.

"One point six two." The woman calls.

I nod.

"One point six five." My bidder calls.

The lady laughs and shakes her head, "I'm out."

"One point six five, once." The auctioneer calls, "One point six five, twice." His voice is loud and echoing through the art gallery. "Last call, one point six five... sold." He slams down his hammer.

Kate shakes her head in disbelief and I put my arm around her, "Look at you go, baby." I whisper. "Congratulations."

"I can't believe it."

"I can. You're amazing."

Kate

"Could there be a more perfect night?" I smile dreamily as we walk hand in hand into our penthouse. We are met with a glass wall overlooking the twinkling lights of Paris.

Elliot's eyes hold mine, he has that look in them.

The one that I love.

His lips take mine as he walks me backwards. "What was so good about it?"

"The art auction, dinner overlooking the Eiffel Tower, a date with the world's hottest man."

He kisses me as he backs me up to the wall, his lips take mine with urgency.

I glance over to see a crystal vase with a huge bunch of red roses sitting on the counter with a white card, "What does the card say?" I ask.

"Suck your husband's cock." He murmurs against my lips.

I giggle because I know in reality it says something desperately romantic about how proud he is of me, he can't help himself.

He does it every auction.

I drop to my knees and unzip his pants, with my eyes locked on his I slide the top of his cock into my mouth, he inhales sharply as he watches on.

His hands grip my hair as we get into a rhythm as he fucks my mouth hard, and no matter how many times I do this, bringing Elliot Miles undone is my favorite thing in the world.

He shudders and I smile around him, "Don't you dare fucking come."

I sit on a stool at the bar and listen to Elliot speak to a man. They are laughing and chatting in fluent French and I have to say that hearing him speak the native language does things to my libido. It fires it up like a blazing volcano.

The man smiles over at me and picks up my hand and kisses the back of it. "Good day, Kate, lovely to meet you."

"You too. Goodbye." I watch as he then goes back to his table.

"Sorry." Elliot smiles as he runs his hand up my leg. "That conversation went longer than I thought."

"How do you know him?"

"He used to be a neighbor of our penthouse here in Paris."

"Oh." I turn and watch the man for a moment, he's suave and handsome and the woman he is with is gorgeous. "What does he do?"

"He owns a record label."

"Really?" I frown, fascinated. "You sure know some interesting people."

"I do." His mischievous eyes hold mine. "You know I married an artist that I had been admiring from afar for years?"

"Did you?"

"I did." He kisses my fingertips. "Although I always knew that I would."

I smirk over at him and lean onto my hand. "Did you really though?"

He takes a sip of his wine. "I actually did, although when I didn't know it was you I was totally confused because reality wasn't matching up with my gut instinct." He frowns. "I have this weird sixth sense thing going on and it's never ever wrong."

I smile dreamily as I listen.

"It's like I already know what is meant for me and what is not." He sips his wine and frowns as if contemplating something. "Like I already know, I'm going to blow hard tonight."

"That's a no-brainer." I giggle. "You blow hard every night."

He raises his glass to me and throws me a sexy wink.

I sip my wine and fall silent as my mind begins to wander; I haven't stopped thinking about his reaction to me wanting to go off the pill.

It was unexpected and it's thrown me.

"What?" he asks.

"What do you mean?"

"What are you thinking about?"

"Nothing."

He raises an eyebrow, ugh, I can't hide anything from this man, he can read me like a book.

"Well it's just...." I spin my wine glass on the table by the stem as I try to articulate my thoughts.

"Just what?"

"Your reaction to me wanting a baby has thrown me a little. I thought...." I shrug. "I thought we were on the same page with this."

His eyes hold mine.

"I'm twenty-nine and you are thirty-six, we are not getting any younger, El."

His eyes glow with a tenderness. "I never said I don't want a baby, only that I don't need one."

"You really think we are not going to be able to have one, don't you?"

He shrugs. "I'm scared of the process, I guess."

"Why?"

"Kate, the contraceptive pill holds your endometriosis at bay. You've had numerous surgeries and also have polycystic ovaries. I watch you nearly die while in so much pain every month, I can't imagine how bad you will suffer if not on the pill."

"*That's* what you're worried about?"

"Of course I worry about it. I don't want you to suffer to give me a baby out of obligation. Fuck that, I would rather you be pain free and happy. I don't need a kid."

I smile as my heart flutters. "I love you."

He leans over and kisses me. "I love you more."

"In a lot of cases, endo improves with pregnancy. Although it may be a little harder to fall in the beginning." I take his hand in mine. "We can do it, I know we can. I want to try."

He exhales heavily.

I smile over at my beautiful husband, so thoughtful and caring. Always putting my needs before his.

"Kate...."

"It's going to be okay, Elliot."

His eyes search mine.

"I know you have a feeling that this isn't going to work out, but I have faith that it will."

"I can't watch you suffer, Kate. I won't let it happen for anything, not even a baby."

"So...." I think for a moment. "We put a time limit on it. If I haven't fallen naturally in three months we go down the IVF route."

He steeples his finger up the side of his face as he listens. "And what then?"

"What do you mean, what then?"

"What's the time limit for IVF?"

"Well, obviously I'll fall on IVF." I smile. "It's a given."

"And in the instance that you don't, what's the time limit?" he asks.

I smile, I know I've nearly got him. "Five years."

"No, I am not wasting five years trying for a baby. One."

"One." I gasp. "One year isn't long enough to give up trying for a baby, four."

He shakes his head. "No. Two."

I smile hopefully. "Three."

He gives me the best come-fuck-me look of all time. "That's a lot of head you have to give."

I giggle. "It is." I run my hand up his thigh and feel his thick quad muscle. "What do you think?"

He exhales heavily. "I think you could talk me into anything, that's what I think."

I smile hopefully. "So can we try?"

His eyes hold mine. "Babe...."

"I'm not going to suffer, I'll be okay, El. I promise you, and if it gets too much we stop. I'm not a fool."

"I know how stubborn you are."

"Can we at least try, it's going to be fun practicing either way?"

He twists his lips as he tries to hold in his smile. "On the condition that you give you me your word. Three years from this date."

"Easy." I smile goofily. "We could have three children in three years from this date."

He winces as he imagines three crying babies and I laugh out loud, I take his hands in mine. "Let's go home and fuck."

He winks. "*This* I can do."

"No anal."

"What?" He frowns.

"We're trying for a baby, anal is off the table for a while."

"Not helping the cause, Kate," he mutters dryly. "Aren't you supposed to be talking me into this not out of it?"

I stand and pick up my bag. "I already did that, let's go home."

Six months later.

Elliot, as serious as all hell, sits at the kitchen table and reads the instructions again.

He holds the needle in his hand as he prepares to give me my first injection. He's been practicing on oranges all week.

Today is the first day of IVF for us.

"Hurry up about it, just jab it in and get it over with."

"You are not a cow, Kate; I'm not just jabbing it in." He frowns as he concentrates on what he's reading.

I take off my T-shirt and present my stomach to him. "Put it in here." I point to a patch of skin.

He twists his lips as he looks over my stomach and then gets up and grabs an ice tray from the freezer.

"What's that for?"

"I don't want to bruise you."

"Since when have you cared about bruising me, have you seen your finger marks on my hips?"

He smirks. "That was your husband who did that, he's a fucking animal. I'm your doctor."

"Ahh, but I like to fuck my doctor like an animal too."

"Stop being a pain-in-the-ass patient or I'm going to throw this needle in like a dart."

I giggle and he puts the needle in position and I turn my head. "Just do it."

I feel the sting as it slides through my skin and I hold my breath as I feel the liquid go in.

"Done."

I exhale in relief, Elliot pulls me down onto his lap and we kiss, his lips linger over mine.

We are full of hope and even more in love than ever.

"Here we go, my hot doctor." I smile against his lips.

His arms tighten around me. "Here we go, my fuckable patient."

———

The phone rings and we hold our breath....

It's been the best month; the hormone injections have turned me into Godzilla but Elliot has been his patient and loving self. Everything is falling into place and I have a good feeling about this. Elliot answers the phone and puts it on speaker.

"Hello, it's Rosemary from the clinic."

"Hi, Rosemary."

"The blood tests are back."

I close my eyes. *Please, please, please.*

"Unfortunately in this instance the test is negative."

My heart sinks.

"Thanks for calling," Elliot replies before hanging up.

Elliot kisses my temple, "Next month, babe."

I smile sadly, I really thought it was this month. "Yep."

"Do you want a coffee?" he asks as he stands.

"Yes please."

He walks off into the kitchen and I stare at the phone and exhale heavily, I can't help but be disappointed.

It's fine. It's just one month...so what? We go again next month.

It's fine.

Six months later.

"Give me the phone and you go outside." Elliot smirks.

I pass him the phone as it rings.

I can't even be in the room for the phone calls anymore; it stresses me out too much and I nearly have a heart attack.

This is the month.

Six rounds of IVF and six disappointments. This one is lucky because it's number seven, our lucky number.

I go outside and go for a walk down to the bottom paddock and visit Humphrey, our ram. He broke one of his horns attacking the fence post so we've been keeping a close eye on him. That will teach him not to be a psychopath.

Gretel is pregnant again; seems Billy just has to look her way and she's up the duff.

If only.

I linger outside with my heart in my throat, I keep looking up to the house expecting to see Elliot come out to find me, because I know if he has good news he will.

But he's not coming...and I know the results would be out by now.

I sit down on a rock and stare out over the farm. My chest is tight with a sense of dread, this is the one thing we cannot control.

And it's fucking hard.

Infertility doesn't discriminate, no matter how in love you are, how much of a great parent you'd make, what you earn or where you live.

It hits you like a truck, steals your heart and makes you feel like a failure.

I want a baby so badly that it hurts.

What if we never get one?

My eyes well with tears and I stare into space, eventually Elliot sits down on the rock beside me.

He doesn't say anything, he doesn't have to.

We both sit on our rock in silence, together but alone, lost in our own world of regret.

Mourning another failed attempt but grateful that we have each other.

This sucks.

Elliot

Jameson puts his head around the door, "You want to grab some lunch."

I exhale heavily, "I can't, I've got to do something."

"Such as?" He walks in, his interest piqued.

I open the top draw to my desk and hold up the specimen jar, "I've got to blow into this fucking cup."

Jameson chuckles, "Sounds romantic."

"Trust me, it's not." I roll my eyes, "I'm sick of this shit."

"Do you want me to bring up some cocky boys for you on your computer?"

I fake a smile, "Gay porn is not going to get the job done."

"Then I'm afraid I can't help you."

"*You* can't." I hear Kate say from the door, "But I can."

"Hi Jay," Kate smiles as she walks in, she's wearing a trench coat and I have a sneaking suspicion that she has nothing on underneath it.

I feel my cock twinge in appreciation.

"Ahh, the calvary has arrived to help me with my errands." I smile as I pull her down onto my lap.

Jameson smirks, "I'll leave you to it."

Kate

I sit on the step.

The sun is rising and Elliot is dressed in his killer suit, coffee in hand walking around the lake.

His gang of ducks waddling behind him.

Every now and then he will stop still as he looks around and he says something to them and I smile as I watch on.

What does he say?

It's always magical here but mornings are something special, it really does become enchanted.

We are so blessed.

Eighteen months later.

The grand ballroom is alive with laughter, we are at a charity ball.

Elliot is wearing a black dinner suit and I am pimped up to the nines, my hair is out and full and I'm in a black sexy dress with sky high stilettos. I used to loathe these things but now not so much, it gives us a chance to get dressed up and go on a fancy date.

Let's face it, anytime Elliot Miles puts on a dinner suit it's a gift to the world.

He runs his hand up my thigh under the table and gives me the look.

He's so fucking gorgeous I can't stand it.

We've had dinner, he's spun me around the dance floor and dessert is just about to be served.

"So when are you two going to have a baby?" the woman across the table asks.

My stomach drops.

And there it is, the question on everyone's lips.

"Not yet," Elliot replies curtly.

We hardly know her. Why does she think it's okay to ask such a personal question?

I fake a smile as my heart sinks. I want to crawl under the table and hide from the world.

Twelve failed rounds of IVF are bad enough to deal with.

But getting asked the question everywhere we go is a hard pill to swallow. Even the paps are weighing in on it now.

When are you having a baby?

A simple, harmless question with no malice intended. The result...a cut so deep that it goes straight to the bone.

If they only knew what was going on behind closed doors.

I can't blame them, it's a question that comes up and perhaps I've even asked someone the same insensitive thing before. It's as if it's a god-given right that everyone gets to choose...and hell, I only wish that were true.

Reality is setting in, this actually may not happen for us, and Elliot's right, I need to prepare myself for it.

My heart is bleeding for every mom that didn't get her baby.

For her dream of a family that didn't come true.

For the dads that never got to go to the mini league game, the Santa Claus they didn't get to play.

My mind goes round in circles, from the highest of highs to the lowest of lows.

Everywhere I go I see them; pregnant woman are everywhere. With their big, beautiful tummies on display. Glowing and gorgeous.

Femininity personified.

And then there's me, a walking nutjob with my hormones all over the place, laughing one minute and crying the next. Hearing a simple song can set me off on a crying tangent for three hours and don't get me started on my raging temper.

I'm up, I'm down, I'm a one-woman fucking circus.

I've never felt like such a failure.

Getting a negative result is bad...but watching Elliot's heart sink is.... worse.

I can feel his disappointment, sense all the words he doesn't say.

It kills me.

It's like we are on this roller coaster to hell, every month we start off optimistic.

Every month ends in disappointment, the cut a little bit deeper, a little bit wider.

An infection that is festering just under the surface.

Elliot says he can't do this anymore, he's had enough.

But I have to be strong, I can't give up, my faith is strong, our happy ending is coming.

It has to.

Elliot

I pinch the skin on Kate's stomach and slide the needle under her skin.

"I'm getting a pro at this." I smirk. "I would have made a great doctor."

Kate bends and kisses my head. "Dr. Love."

I smile and stare up at Kate and sit back on my feet. "The last injection."

She nods and smiles sadly. "I know."

Twenty-four rounds of IVF over three years.

All failed.

This is our last try.

They call it unexplained infertility.

The eggs are great, the sperm is good, it goes great in a test tube but as soon as the embryo is transplanted it doesn't take.

There is no reason.

I think it would be easier to take if there was, because then we would know what we were up against and we could fix it.

But this....

I stand and pull Kate to me for a hug, I hold her tight. "This is the last time, sweetheart."

She nods through tears. "I know. I have faith it's going to work out this time, El." She smiles into my shoulder.

I squeeze her harder.

I wish I did.

"If this doesn't work out, we move on with our lives, Kate. We can't do this forever."

"I know, baby." She nods. "I gave you my word, this is it."

"I have to go to work." I sigh.

She gives me a lopsided smile as she straightens my tie. "Have a good day, Dr. Love."

"I will." I kiss her softly. "Paint me something amazing today."

She smiles. "Don't I always?"

I kiss her again and my hands go to her behind. "You do, actually."

"Love you."

"Love you too."

I make my way out to the car and drive down the winding driveway.

My mind is running a million miles per minute.

I think I'm going to book a long vacation for the end of the month.

I guess it's going to go one of two ways, we will either be celebrating the start of our new life or commiserating as we close the door on a dream.

Either way, we need a fresh start.

It's time to start living again.

Kate

My phone buzzes in my bag and I dig it out, a familiar name lights up the screen.

Emily

"Hi, babe."

"Hey, how are you feeling?"

"Nervous." I hunch my shoulders up. Emily, my sister-in-law, has become my rock.

I'm close to all my sisters-in-law, but I have a special bond with Em. We are probably the most alike and she's become one of my best friends, we speak every day.

"You should hear soon, right?"

"Yep."

"Are you going to do a test today?"

"No, I'm going to wait until they call me. I just...." I exhale heavily. "I'm so nervous."

"It's going to be positive; I know it."

I nod. "Yes, positive thoughts." I smile hopefully. "You're right."

"Call me tomorrow."

"Okay."

"How's Elliot?" she asks.

"Quiet."

"Jeez."

"It will be fine, either way, we'll be fine." I smile hopefully.

"Yeah, you're right. You will. It's going to be fine. Love you."

"You too, bye."

I wake to a deep ache in my stomach and I roll onto my back and close my eyes.

No....

My period is coming.

I look over to Elliot who is sound asleep beside me and then back up at the ceiling.

So close....

A hot tear rolls down my face and into my ear.

I get a vision of what our family could have been....

I screw up my face in tears and roll into a fetal position on my side.

My heart aches.

How do you let go of a dream?

I should wake Elliot and tell him but what's the point.

I'll let him sleep.

I get up and go to the bathroom and get out a sanitary pad and stare at it in my hand, I screw up my face in tears.

I slide down the tiles and sit on the floor. In the darkness, alone....

I sob in silence.

Elliot

I roll over and put my arm out to Kate, her side of the bed is empty. I sit up onto my elbows. "Kate?" I call.

Silence....

"Kate?" I get out of bed and go in search of her. "Kate?" I walk into the bathroom and see a pack of her sanitary pads on the counter and my heart drops.

Fuck.

I walk back into the bedroom and sit on the bed, I put my head into my hands.

I don't know how to make this better.

For a long time I sit, mustering up the courage to find her. Trying to think of the right thing to say when I do.

We are nothing special, this happens to a lot of people, I know that.

It's just a lot more real when you go through it.

How long has she known?

Why didn't she wake me? Is this all about her, is it?

Suddenly I'm angry.

I march downstairs and out to the art studio. As I get closer I can hear loud music playing. Heavy metal shit music, I've never heard her play this before.

I frown. What's going on here? I slide open the big barn door to see her splatting paint all over the painting she's been working on for weeks.

Ruining it.

"What the fuck are you doing?" I scream as my heart hammers in my chest.

"Getting on with it," she yells over the horrendous music.

"By ruining your painting?"

"It's *my* painting."

I storm over and turn off the music. "Why the fuck didn't you wake me?" I yell.

"So I didn't have to see the disappointment on your face even earlier than I have to," she cries as if losing control.

I glare at her. "It's all about you...isn't it?" I sneer.

"Are you happy now?" she cries through tears. "Are you fucking happy, Elliot?"

"The fuck is that supposed to mean?"

"You said all along that this was going to happen. Are you happy that—" she holds her fingers up to air quote herself, "—your destiny has called, Congratulations Elliot, you got it right again. You never wanted a baby anyway. Admit it."

I screw up my face in disgust. "Don't you dare."

"Do what. Speak the truth?"

"Go to hell."

"I'm already there," she screams like a mad woman; she turns and picks up a whole tin of paint and hurls it at the canvas. "*Get out.*"

"Fuck. You." I turn and march back to the house, I hear the heavy metal music blast back on.

Adrenaline is pumping through my body as I shower and get ready for work.

I am not being her punching bag for this fucking bullshit. I collect my things and storm to my car; I tear down the driveway.

I get to the T-intersection at the bottom of the driveway and come to a stop, I close my eyes, this morning couldn't have gone any worse.

This is fucked.

Kate

Six days and six nights....

That's how long since Elliot and I have spoken.

We both apologized for being horrible that morning, but that's about it. The house has been quiet and pensive.

We sit at the dining table and eat in silence, no words, no laughter, just animosity swimming between us. It's better this way, I know that if we're nice to each other we are both going to fall apart.

It's easier being angry.

"We go to New York tomorrow for Tristan's birthday, remember?" Elliot sighs.

"Yes." I nod, it's the last place I want to be, but I know it will cheer me up to see everyone. I'm trying to snap myself out of this mood but I just don't seem to be able to.

We go away next week so I'm hoping we both turn the corner; we've never fought like this.

Elliot collects my plate with his and washes them both up, he walks past me and puts his hand on my shoulder. "Good night, Kate."

"Good night."

I watch him disappear upstairs and I glance at my watch: 8 p.m. He'd rather go to bed than have to talk to me.

I exhale heavily, great.

New York.

The table is alive with chatter and laughter, family always cheers me up.

The kids are climbing all over the chairs, drinks are spilling and everything is chaos.

I'm so glad we came. After spending the afternoon with Emily I feel so much better, more like myself.

Elliot is sitting beside me and we still haven't spoken but I know it's going to be okay; we just needed some alone time to process everything.

It's been a week from hell.

Our little family is staying at two, and slowly but surely I'm coming to grips with it.

Deep down I know Elliot is right, we can't go on like this.

It's no way to live.

I'm going to let go of any preconceived ideas of what my life should be. Throw myself into painting and our farm and enjoy my beautiful man.

Because he deserves my best.

"We've got some news," Tristan announces.

The table falls silent.

"Claire's pregnant."

What?

My heart stops and I fake a smile.

"Six kids." Christopher gasps. "Jesus, you two are serial breeders."

The table erupts into congratulations and Emily's sympathetic eyes flick to me.

"Congratulations." I smile. "That's fantastic news."

Elliot takes my hand under the table and links his fingers through mine.

His act of kindness slays my bravado and I feel the tears welling behind my eyes.

Stop it.

He squeezes my hand as a silent comfort.

Don't cry.

This is a happy announcement and I am happy for them, really I am. The other pregnancy announcements from Claire and Emily haven't worried me before.

I roll my lips.

I just wish they were congratulating Elliot, calling him a serial breeder.

Don't cry.

I can feel the hot caustic tears building and I need them to go to hell. I will not make this about me and cause a scene.

This is exciting, a baby is a gift.

Don't cry.

"I'm just going to the bathroom," I whisper, I get up and near run to the disabled bathroom, I close the door behind me.

They get six, *we don't even get one.*

I lean my forehead on the back of the door, my open hands hold me up, my heartbeat sounding in my ears, the pain in my chest so sharp that I screw up my face in pain. Poisonous, jealous tears run down my face.

My breath quivers as I inhale, trying desperately to calm myself down.

I don't want to be this person; this isn't who I am.

"Kate." I hear Emily's voice. "Where are you, babe?"

I screw up my face even more, the snot is running down my face. "I'm sorry," I whisper. "I'll be out in a moment." I wipe my eyes. "I'll meet you back out there."

"Let me in."

"I'm fine, Em."

"Open the fucking door."

I open the door to see Emily, Claire and Hayden, and I want the earth to swallow me up. "I'm so sorry," I whisper, the tears starting again.

Claire pulls me into a hug. "I'm so sorry, sweetie, I didn't realize."

"I don't want to be this person." I whisper, embarrassed.

"You have every right to be upset," Claire comforts me. "Howl to the moon."

I smile, grateful for her kindness. "I've ruined everything."

"No you haven't."

Emily passes me tissues and I wipe my eyes. "God, I'm an idiot making this about me, I'm so sorry."

"Don't be silly, we're family." Emily puts her arm around me. "We've got you; your heartache is our heartache."

The tears well again. "Don't be nice to me." I laugh. "It makes me psychotic."

We all laugh and eventually we make our way back to the table.

Everyone is silent, unsure to what to say.

"Sorry." I sit down, mortified, "My behavior is inexcusable."

Elliot puts his arm around me and kisses my temple as he pulls me close.

"So as you already know," I say as I look around the table, "Elliot and I have been struggling with fertility for a long time, it's not working and we've finally accepted that we are unable to have a baby."

The table sits still as they listen.

"As of this week we've officially stopped trying. There will be no children for us and it's been hard to come to that decision. It's new and it's raw and I really *am* so happy for you guys." I smile through tears.

Elliot rolls his lips as he stares at the table, unable to make eye contact with anyone.

The table falls silent, unsure what to say.

"I'm so sorry, guys," Jameson whispers.

"We're going to get going." Elliot stands, unable to have this conversation. "Sorry to be on a downer." He shakes Tristan's hand. "Happy for you, buddy." He kisses Claire. "Congrats."

"I'm sorry for ruining the night," I say, embarrassed. "I promise I'll get my shit together and be better company next time."

"You have not ruined the night," Claire gasps.

To the loud goodbyes, Elliot puts his arm around me and we leave and make our way out of the restaurant. And, for the first time, we fall apart together.

———

The suns heat dances across my skin.

From my place on the deckchair I look out over the sea, my eyes roam across the beautiful surroundings and then over to my sleeping man.

Elliot and I are in Capri, Italy.

Staying in the most beautiful waterfront villa, heaven on earth.

He organized this trip for us last month to either be celebrating or drying our tears.

Although, I'm not sure if they're dry yet, maybe they never will.

If I'm honest, it's kind of just sinking in.

It seems so crazy that all of our energy over the last three years has been focused on getting pregnant, somehow in amongst it, we kind of forgot how to just be us.

But it feels like we've turned the corner.

Our love for each other is stronger than ever and our life might not be perfect.

But it's ours.

We're in this together and it's going to be okay.

And Elliot's right, we don't need a child to complete us. I mean, it would have been nice but we can't lose ourselves in the search of something else.

He's still Elliot Miles and I'm still Kate Miles, we're still happily married.

Still smart asses, still hot as fuck for each other and damn it, I'm not going to waste one more minute forgetting who I am and what I have in this life.

Because I have him, *and he is everything.*

Elliot rolls onto his side and runs his hand up my thigh, "Want a Margarita babe?"

"Yeah." I smile, "Why not? Make it two."

Five months later.

I put the finishing touches on the chicken. "El," I call. "Can you get the wine from the cellar?"

"Already got it."

I carry the chicken out and proudly place it in the middle of the dining table.

"This looks frigging incredible." Emily smiles as she looks around the table.

She and Jameson and the kids have come to stay with us for the week, we have had so many laughs.

The kids ate earlier and are watching a movie in the living room.

Jameson pours us four glasses of wine and we all sit at the table and begin to serve out our meals.

"So.... There's something we wanted to talk to you about," Jameson says casually as he dishes out his chicken, he seems distracted and keeps loading it onto his plate.

"Don't eat all the fucking chicken." Elliot snatches the tongs from him.

"We were thinking...." His voice trails off, causing Elliot and me to look up at him.

"Did it hurt?" Elliot mutters dryly. "Spit it out."

"We want Emily to be your surrogate."

My knife and fork hit the plate with a clang. "What?"

"I've had four kids. James, Imogen and Alexander are older now and with Lauren we are complete. My uterus can hold another pregnancy and I have easy labors," Emily says. "I can do this for you guys. Let us do this for you."

The earth spins beneath me.

Elliot stares at her, shocked to his core.

"I couldn't...."

"Yes you could." Jameson cuts me off. "I know if the shoe was on the other foot, you would do it for us."

We stay silent, unsure what to say.

"We all know that we couldn't trust a stranger to be a surrogate, it's too risky," Jameson continues. "Let us do this for you."

Elliot's eyes search his.

"Your embryo implanted into Emily's uterus; it will be your child."

"I'll just be the oven." Emily smiles as she takes my hand over the table. "We can do this, guys, it's at least worth a try."

Tears well in my eyes. "This is the most selfless act of love I've ever heard of. Thank you so much for the offer...but..."

"It's worth a shot." Elliot cuts me off. "Kate...let's think on it before you dismiss it." He smiles softly at me over the table and for the first time in a long time.

Hope has returned.

Elliot

The phone rings on my nightstand and I wake with a start, I glance at the clock: 2am.

Fuck.

I scramble to answer it, "Hey."

Jameson's deep voice sounds down the phone, "She's in labor."

My heart drops, "Is she okay?"

Kate sits up with a start, "What's happening?" She mouths.

"Yeah, she's a pro at this." Jameson replies. "Been going for about an hour, she's ready to go to the hospital. I've called ahead, they are expecting us."

My stomach twists into knots, this is it. Emily is nine months pregnant with our baby, tonight's the night.

"Okay, meet you there."

"Alright."

He hangs up but I stay on the line, because while I stay here on the phone nothing can go wrong.

"What's happening?" Kate asks.

I need a minute.

"Emily is in labor. Have a shower babe, then we will head down to the hospital."

"Okay." Kate gets into the shower and I march to the guest bathroom and throw up.

Violently.

If something goes wrong, I swear to god........

I'm bent over the toilet and Kate's reassuring hand goes to my back, "It's going to be okay, babe."

I nod, unable to say anything. Barely able to breathe.

"Relax."

I nod, feeling stupid. Poor Emily is going through labor and I'm over here throwing up in sympathy like a wimp.

Kate quickly showers while I try to pull myself together and half an hour later we arrive at the hospital.

It's already been arranged that we can go into the birthing suite and we're ushered straight through.

We walk into the room and Jameson's face lights up, "Hey, here they are." He's calm and relaxed, obviously a pro at this too.

"Hi," Em smiles.

Emily and Kate hug.

I kiss Emily on the cheek and push the hair back from her face, "Are you okay?"

"Yeah." She smiles, she screws up her face, "Here comes another one."

I step out of the way and as Emily pants, the room spins, my panic sets in.

Jameson holds her hand and talks calmly to her, she gets through the contraction and nerves roll my stomach, I'm going to throw up again.

What the fuck?

"I'm sorry guys, I just …. I don't think I can watch Em go through this."

Jameson chuckles. "She's okay."

"No." I shake my head, "This is….. you need to be here with her, I can't ….. this is not for me…. Emily is….. "

"It's okay Elliot." Em smiles.

"I'll wait outside."

Kates eyes search mine, "Are you sure?"

I nod, "I'll be just outside that door." I kiss her, and then Emily and hug Jameson.

Then I run outside and throw up again.

I pace up and down the corridor.

Four hours, four hours of a literal hell.

Poor Emily.

I don't know what the fuck is going on in there but it's taking forever.

The door bursts open and Jameson comes into view.

"Come, last push."

"What?" I gasp wide-eyed.

He grabs me and drags me into the room, "Stand up that end." He positions me behind Emily and I stand still, frozen on the spot.

"Last push Emily." The midwife says, "Let's do this."

Emily strains and pushes and I put my hands over my mouth.

Oh my fucking god.

"That's it, baby." Jameson smiles, "That's it, it's coming."

The baby slides out and my eyes widen, the doctor picks it up and rolls it over.

"It's a little girl."

"Waaaaaa." The baby screams.

My vision blurs, and Kate starts to cry.

Emily and Jameson too.

The nurse wraps the baby and holds it up, "Pass her to her mom and dad." Emily smiles.

The nurse passes her to Kate and I screw up my face in tears as I put my arms around the two of them.

"Thank you, thank you." I whisper.

The whole room is crying.

"Elliot." Kate sobs, "Look at her." She strokes her hair, "I knew you'd come baby girl. I always had faith." She passes her to me and I stare down at the perfect little baby.

She has dark hair with fine features like Kate.

Perfection.

"What are you going to call her?" Jameson asks.

And in that moment, I just know.

"I have the perfect name." I smile as I look down at her in wonder.

"What is it?" Kate whispers as she puts her arm around the both of us.

"Something you never lost sight of."

Kate frowns.

"Faith."

Kate screws up her face in tears. "That's the perfect name," She whispers.

I kiss her tiny forehead, "Her name is Faith."

THE DO-OVER EPILOGUE

THE MILES HIGH CLUB

1

THE DO-OVER EPILOGUE

Hayden

I LISTEN to Christopher show Eddie around his new bedroom as I look around mine.

A million emotions all rushing to the surface at once.

Love, fear...relief.

Excitement.

A farm, our very own farm. And not just any farm, the most perfect place in the world, and Christopher can drive to work from here. I can run cattle and homeschool Eddie, there are so many possibilities for us all to be happy here.

The perfect solution.

I walk up the hall to see Christopher hugging Eddie and my eyes fill with tears, what must it be like to see this day through his eyes?

"Hey." I smile through tears as I walk into Eddie's bedroom.

"Not you too." Christopher rolls his eyes. "Why are you all crying?"

"This is a happy day." I smile.

"Yeah well, it might not be so happy if I get eaten by a wolf." He sighs as he flops onto the bed. "We need to call the person to eradicate that."

"Eradicate what?"

"Wolves, Hayden." He rolls his eyes as if I'm stupid. "What else would I be talking about?"

"You're actually serious?" I gasp in surprise. "There are no wolves in the United Kingdom, Christopher, aren't you supposed to know this?"

"We did hear something growl," Eddie replies, seemingly convinced too. "Something *is* out there, Hazen."

"Listen wimps." I pull back the blankets on Eddie's bed. "Tomorrow I'm going to check it all out and make sure it's safe for you two yellowbellies."

"Eddie and I have never pretended to be farm boys, Hayden. We're city slickers, aren't we, Eddie." He bumps Eddie's shoulder with his.

Eddie smiles goofily with a nod.

"Oh, and there's a house down on the bottom paddocks for your parents," Christopher says casually as if he just remembered. "And another broken-down house on another faraway paddock in real bumfuck nowhere that we will fix up as a guesthouse one day."

I stop still. "What? There's a house for my parents?"

"Uh-huh," He puts his hands on his hips as if proud of himself, "They can come whenever it suits them, even move here if they want."

My eyes well with tears again. "I can't believe this, Christopher, you've done all this for me?"

He pulls me close and kisses my lips, "I want you to be happy, Grumps."

"This is going to be a big adjustment for you boys." I look between them.

"We can hack it. Can't we, Ed?"

My heart sinks. "I don't want you to hack it, I want you to love it."

Christopher puts his arm around Eddie and pulls him close. "As long as we're all together, everything is going to be alright. And you want to be a farm girl, so we are going to love it."

"Do you promise?" I ask hopefully.

"Well it better be," Eddie mutters dryly. "You're getting married now, remember?"

I giggle and look down at the ring on my finger as I sit on the bed, the boys sit down either side of me. "I can't believe it." I look up to Eddie. "We have so much to do, buddy, we have to sort our new house out and organize a wedding and grocery shop and oh, do we have a tractor?"

Christopher frowns. "Calm down. What is it with you and fucking tractors? Do you watch tractor porn?"

We all fall silent as our minds individually race off on tangents.

"Big few days," Christopher eventually says.

"Why, what are we doing?"

"Well." He thinks for a moment. "Tomorrow we can look around the farm and then we're going to take Eddie to London and show him around."

Eddie's eyes light up. "Really?"

"And buy some furniture while we are there," Christopher says really quickly in hope that Eddie didn't hear it.

"I don't need furniture." I sigh dreamily. "I have everything I want right here in this room."

Christopher twists his lips. "Hate to burst your bubble,

Grumps, but you're going to get sick of sitting on the floor real quick."

I giggle. "This is true."

We fall silent again.

"What do you think, Eddie?" Christopher slaps him on the back. "Do you like your new home?"

Eddie nods, he's so overwhelmed.

I am too, actually.

This is a dream come true.

"I'm so happy." I smile over at my beautiful man. "Like stupidly happy."

Christopher's eyes darken and then drop to my lips, he gives me the best come-fuck-me look of all time.

"Bedtime," he mouths.

My skin prickles with excitement, it's been way too long without him.

"You should probably put a movie on your iPad while you're falling asleep," Christopher tells Eddie. "Just so...you know, you don't hear the farm animals."

I roll my lips to hide my smile. *There's only one animal here.*

"Would that be alright?" Eddie looks between us. "It won't keep you up?"

Christopher widens his eyes at me. "I'm already up."

Behave.

Eddie gets up and grabs his iPad and begins to scroll through. "Oh." He frowns. "I don't have internet."

"Hot spot from my phone." Christopher hands his phone straight over and hooks it up. He'll do anything not to be heard tonight. "What movie do you want to watch?" he asks as he peruses the choices. "Get something that will really block out those animals. They are crazy loud."

I giggle and kiss Eddie's forehead. "I'll leave you two to it, good night, baby."

Eddie smiles up at me. "Good night, Hazen."

I glance back from the door and watch Christopher and Eddie scroll through Netflix on the iPad and my heart swells.

I'm so happy I could burst.

I walk in and look around the master bedroom, it's small and cozy with no en-suite bathroom, so unlike Christopher's penthouse in London.

It's a typical old farmhouse and out of scale to an extent. Some rooms are oversized and then the ones you think would be big are much smaller. Like the stairway and hallway are wide and grand, but then the master bedroom is smallish.

Not that I'm complaining, it's homely and perfectly sized for us.

I could live in a tent on this property and be as happy as a pig in mud.

I unzip my suitcase and then, overwhelmed, I sit on the bed and look around.

I can't believe today has happened.

He did all this for me...for us, so that we could both be happy.

The ultimate compromise.

Emotion overwhelms me and the happy tears well in my eyes.

Christopher walks in and his face falls. "Hey, what's wrong?"

The lump in my throat is so big. "Nothing is wrong, everything is right."

"Why are you crying?" He brushes the hair back from my forehead.

"I'm just so happy."

He smiles softly, his eyes filled with a tender glow, and he cups my face in his hand. "I died a little every day being away from you," he whispers.

I screw up my face in tears. "Me too."

"Don't leave me again."

"I won't." I kiss his big, beautiful lips, my tears of relief falling down onto my cheeks. "I'll never be away from you again; I can't stand it."

"Sshh," he whispers against my lips. "We're together now. It's over, babe." I hug him tight, so tight that I might actually crush him.

"The first thing we need to do is get soundproofing in these fucking walls," he says. "How am I supposed to fuck you like I want to when I have to be quiet?"

I giggle.

"I'm not even joking," he mutters dryly as he stands and pulls me up by the hand. "And we need an en-suite bathroom."

"The house is perfect as it is."

"Hayden," he says sternly. "I love you, but in all seriousness, if we're going to live out here in Bumfuck Nowhere, the house needs some major renovating."

He grabs two towels out of the suitcase he has with him.

"Such as?"

"These bedrooms all doubled in size, new bathrooms and kitchen." He looks around at the floral wallpaper and points at it. "That has got to go. New every fucking thing. You can do whatever you want to this farm, it's your home. The farming part and cows and all of that stuff is all yours. But I am insisting on fixing up this dump of a house...with yours and Eddie's input of course."

I imagine us planning and renovating and building up our cattle and the life we will live and I smile hopefully. "It sounds like so much fun."

"You're not all there, are you?" He frowns down at me as he takes me into his arms.

"No, but I'm all here."

He kisses me softly as he smiles against my lips. "I love you."

"I love you."

"Mrs. Miles."

"Oh my god." I giggle as I hold up my hand to look at my ring.

"Do you like it?" he asks. "We can change it to something you like better if you want?"

"I love it." I pull him closer. "It, this house, and you...are perfect."

His hands trail down to my behind and he pulls me onto his large erection. "Get in the shower, we're about to break some tiles."

———

"Ahhhhchoooooooo."

I wake with a start.

"Achoo, achoo, achoo."

I sit up, half asleep. "Huh."

"Ahhhhchooooooo." Someone sneezes from downstairs. "Ahhhhchooooooo, Ahhhhchooooooo."

"What the hell?" I get out of bed and throw my robe on and make my way downstairs. Someone is having some kind of crazy sneezing attack.

"Ahhhhchooooooo, Ahhhhchooooooo. Stop fucking laughing," Christopher whispers angrily.

"Stop sneezing like an idiot then," Eddie fires back.

"You think I want to be sneezing like a motherfucker? Newsflash. No I don't, Eduardo."

I come around the corner to see Christopher, sneezing his head off, his eyes are swollen and red and he has toilet paper blowing his nose.

"What's happening?" I frown.

"I'm having some kind of situation," Christopher says as he blows his nose hard. "Ahhhhchooooooo, Ahhhh-chooooooo."

I look around. "Oh, it's the flowers."

"What?"

"The flowers are giving you hay fever".

"Hay fever." Eddie frowns. "But there isn't any hay."

"It's the pollen from all the flowers," I tell them, I pick up two vases of flowers and take them out to the front veranda. "Eddie, help me take them out of the house. He's allergic."

"Ahhhhchooooooo, Ahhhhchooooooo... Ahhhh-chooooooo, Ahhhhchooooooo."

I giggle as I continue to carry the vases outside, and Eddie helps too.

"Why did you buy so many?" Eddie huffs.

"To be romantic, dipshit. Ahhhhchooooooo, Ahhhh-chooooooo...Ahhhhchooooooo, Ahhhhchooooooo."

"Get out of the house while we carry them out, Eddie, open all the windows to let the pollen out," I tell them. "Christopher, drive to the pharmacy and grab some antihis-tamines."

"Where's the pharmacy? Ahhhhchooooooo," he sniffles.

"I don't know, but you need to find one."

He grabs his keys, "It's probably a trek wherever it is, nowhere is close now that we live out here in the boondocks."

"Why are you so dramatic?"

"Because I'm dying here, Hayden, that's fucking why?" He coughs in an overdramatic way, "I'm going into anaphylactic shock now and I'm guessing the nearest hospital isn't close."

"Oh my god." I roll my eyes. "Go with him, Eddie, so you can revive the big baby if he dies."

Eddie and Christopher get into the car and disappear down the driveway and I look around at the living room full of flowers, I didn't even take a photo of his over-the-top grand gesture. There must be at least one hundred bunches of roses here.

I run upstairs and grab my phone; I need to get this on film.

An hour and a half later I sit on the front veranda steps with a cup of tea, I have no idea where they went to buy the antihistamines but I'm thinking it must have been all the way back to Spain.

I'm itching to look around the property but I want them to be with me when I do the tour.

"God's sakes, hurry up."

What if he really did go into anaphylaxis?

He didn't, he's just overdramatic.

I can hear the wind in the trees and the bubbling stream in the distance and I don't think I've ever appreciated being surrounded by nature as much as I do in this moment.

Our home.

I wanted to wait for Christopher to get here to call my

parents, but I can't wait any longer. I FaceTime a group chat to both of their phones.

"Hello." My mom's beautiful face comes into view.

The screen spins around as my dad struggles to answer. "That you, Hayden?" he says in his gruff voice.

"Hi guys." I beam.

"You arrived safely then, love?" Mom asks.

"Yes, sorry I didn't message last night. It was so hectic once we landed."

"Is Eddie okay?" asks Mom.

"He's great. I'm great, everything is so great."

Dad frowns. "What's so great about it?"

"Well..." I swallow the nervous lump in my throat. "Christopher asked me to marry him and he bought us a farm to live in just outside of London that I can run my own cattle on and there's a house on the property for you," I blurt out in a rush.

Mom's face lights up. "Darling, that's wonderful."

Dad's face stays somber.

"And its three hundred and fifty acres of the most beautiful land," I gush.

Dad nods and my heart sinks, I can see the disappointment in his face, he really wanted me to come home and live permanently.

"You're not happy, Dad?"

He shrugs. "I'm happy if you're happy."

"I am." Tears well in my eyes, what is it with all these tears? "I tried to live without him, Dad, and I couldn't. We belong together and this is his way of making me happy and I can come home anytime I want. I'm not tied here."

He nods. "I'm happy for you. Happier for Christopher because he won the lottery."

"I did too, Dad."

"I know, he's a good man."

"So can you come over?"

"When?"

"Tomorrow?"

Mom chuckles. "Not yet this month, love. I have too many cows in calf, Hayden. We'll have to wait a bit."

"I'll get to work renovating your house." I beam. "I'm so excited."

"Me too," laughs Mom.

I hear the car coming up the driveway. "I've got to go, I'll send you some pictures and call you later. Love you."

"Love you too, bye, darling."

Christopher and Eddie get out of the car, they're carrying grocery bags.

"What took you so long, where did you go?" I ask as I meet them on the driveway.

"To the closest shop," Christopher says, deadpan.

I giggle, his sneezing seems to have stopped at least.

"He's not joking," Eddie whispers. "But we did get lost on the way back and Christopher left his phone at home and I had no internet so we had no maps."

"Oh." I giggle as I look over to Christopher. "How are you feeling?"

"Better."

"He took four of the tablets," Eddie tells me.

"Four?" I gasp.

"He was only supposed to take one."

"Christopher, that's so irresponsible," I scold him.

"I'm alive." He does an overexaggerated bow.

"I've been waiting for you to get back before I look around."

He chuckles and takes my hand in his. "Come then. Dump the groceries on the veranda, we've got looking to do."

For the next hour, Eddie, Christopher and I walk around the heavenly property. Paddock after green paddock, stone sheds and stables. Perfect fencing and streams. The two guesthouses are run down but will be easy to fix up.

"Oh Christopher, this is just so beautiful." I sigh with my hand on my heart. "I could never have imagined that something like this would ever be ours." I put my arm around Eddie's shoulders to pull him closer to me. "Could you have ever dreamed that we would live here, Eddie?"

"Nope."

Christopher smiles as he looks around. "It is beautiful, isn't it?"

"We're going to be so happy here."

"Once we get the wolf situation checked out. Let's go back to the house."

"You didn't show her yet," Eddie reminds him softly.

Christopher frowns in question.

"You know, the thing." Eddie raises an eyebrow. "The surprise thing."

"Oh... Our big-ticket item." Christopher laughs. "Yes, I almost forgot."

"What thing?" I frown.

We walk back down to the other side of the hill to see a huge barn and Christopher opens the doors proudly, "Ta-da."

My mouth falls open. "Oh my god."

A tractor, the most beautiful red tractor you have ever seen.

I climb up to find the keys are in the ignition, and I start her up. She roars and I laugh out loud.

Christopher and Eddie roll their eyes at each other, but I

don't care. I drive straight past them and out of the barn and down over the paddock.

"Are you coming back to the house?" Christopher calls after me.

"Later." I wave as I drive. "I love you," I call.

"Watch out for wolves," Eddie calls.

I laugh as I wave, this is the best day of my life.

Who cares about wolves when you have a big red tractor?

———

I glance at the maps on my phone. "It says it's just up here."

"Here? Are you sure?" Christopher frowns over at me. "What furniture shop is this anyway?"

Eddie is still peering out the car window in awe, we are in London for the day and Eddie's eyes are the size of saucers.

"Yes, here it is." I gesture to the driveway and parking lot. "Turn in here."

Christopher frowns and pulls in. "This is a thrift shop."

"I know." I open the door and climb out of the car.

"Don't get out, Eddie," I hear Christopher instruct him. "We are not getting furniture here. She's gone fucking mad."

I walk around to the driver's side where Christopher is looking at me deadpan through the window, I tap on it and he winds the window down. "We are not buying furniture here, Hayden. Get it out of your head right fucking now."

"Not our forever furniture. Just our right now furniture."

He screws up his face as if I'm from Mars. "Not *any* furniture."

"I thought you said we were planning the house out with an architect and doing major changes."

"We are."

173

"So what's the point of buying expensive furniture now when we have no idea what we eventually want?"

"We buy decent furniture now and we buy expensive furniture then." He glances into the back seat. "Eddie, we don't want crap furniture, do we?"

Eddie shrugs as he looks between us, wisely staying silent.

"Look." I open his car door. "It takes weeks for furniture to arrive and I want to house-train our baby animals before it gets here. This furniture will do for a month or two. Get out of the car," I demand.

"Baby animals?" Christopher scoffs. "We are not having fucking ducks, Hayden, forget that right now. My brother has evil ducks and they plot my murder every time I see them. And what makes you think we are getting baby animals anyway? I never agreed to any of this."

"Because it's a farm."

"So?"

"So it wouldn't be a farm without animals, would it?"

My eyes flick to Eddie who is holding in a smile.

"Eddie, do you want a puppy of your very own?"

Eddie's eyes widen. "Are you serious?"

"Aha, and we need some cats."

"No way in hell," Christopher explodes. "I am not having a cat piss on my things. Absolutely no fucking way."

"Shut up, already." I grab his hand and pull him out of the car and into the store. Christopher's face screws up as if disgusted and I roll my lips to hide my smile. The building has that very distinct secondhand furniture scent.

There are rows after rows of couches and armchairs. Dining tables and bedframes. Everything but the kitchen sink and then some.

Christopher's arms are crossed as he walks through the aisles. "There is nothing here for us, let's go."

"Eddie, pick an armchair for your room and two for the living area," I say. "I'll pick some couches."

Christopher's eyes widen in horror. "What do you mean? They have to match each other."

"Why?"

"Because it's the civilized human fucking law, Hayden."

"Will you stop being such a snob."

"I am not a snob," he barks.

"Sure sound like one," Eddie mutters under his breath.

"I'll make a deal with you," I say to Christopher. "We pick the chairs and dining suite from here and you can choose and buy new mats for the rooms to bring everything together."

Christopher's eyebrow rises as if a little interested. "What kind of rugs?"

"Nice ones."

"Hmm." He walks around. "And what about artwork?"

"Yes, you can pick the artwork."

He twists his lips. "And I'm buying the electronics. I'm not having a fossil television."

"Fine."

"I'll wait in the car then," he says casually.

"Why?"

"Because I can't bear to witness the atrocities that you are about to purchase."

"No you don't. You stay right there. We are picking this stuff out together; this house has to be a little bit of all of us. I want the house colorful and eclectic with equal parts of the three of us." I look around. "Eddie, why don't you pick out anything you like, stuff that reminds you of Spain."

Eddie's eyes light up. "Spain?"

"Yes. You're Spanish, we need to celebrate that. Just because we live in London does not make you any less Spanish."

Christopher smiles over at Eddie as if finally under-standing what I'm trying to do here. If the house is all fancy and Miles like, Eddie and I won't feel at home, we need to ease into this money thing.

"Okay," Christopher says with a newfound enthusiasm. "What about this lamp?" He holds it up, the lampshade is made of stained glass and bright and happy.

Eddie's eyes light up in delight.

"I like it." I smirk, not really, but who cares, they do.

"Okay." Christopher smiles, proud of himself, we continue to keep looking.

"What about this chair?" Eddie says, it's purple and made from checked velvet.

Christopher's lip curls in disgust as he looks it over.

"I love it," I lie. "It would be perfect for your bedroom."

"It would, wouldn't it?" Eddie gushes.

"Go and check out the drawers over in the corner," I tell him. "Maybe we could buy some paint and paint them a nice color too."

"Oh, good idea." Eddie takes off in the direction of the drawers, he almost runs there he's so excited.

Christopher leans in close. "That is the worst fucking chair I have ever seen," he whispers.

"Sshh," I whisper back. "It's for his room, not yours."

"Don't even think about painting those drawers purple, a man has his limits." He leans in again. "For the record, no serial killer chairs are going in our bedroom so don't get any dumb ideas."

"Okay."

"Our bedroom is going to be as bougie as fuck," he mutters.

"Okay."

"With lots of fucking in it."

I smirk as I keep looking, of course there will be. "Can't forget that."

"And war bunker soundproofing in the walls," he adds.

I imagine Christopher soundproofing everything so that we can have loud sex and I get the giggles. "Shut up and keep looking, you sex maniac idiot."

Over the next two hours, we pick three couches and four armchairs, none of them match but the colors kind of go together, six eclectic lamps, a coffee table and three small square corner tables. A huge old oval dining table with ten eclectic chairs, the chairs aren't a set but are all made of the same kind of oak that the table is. I love that they're all different, it reminds me of home. I'm not telling Christopher this yet but that's staying forever, I am totally in love with this dining suite. A beautiful dinner set for twenty, it's pastel colors with tiny pretty flowers all over, I'm quite sure it's going to be a collector's item one day, so, so perfect.

The cashier rings up our purchases. "When could you deliver them?" I ask.

He looks up the truck run. "You're in luck, we have room on tomorrow's load. We can load them this afternoon and drop them to your place first thing in the morning."

Eddie's eyes light up and he practically bounces on the spot. "That's so great," he stammers as his eyes flick to us. "Isn't it, Christo?"

"It sure is." Christopher's eyes twinkle with a certain

something as he slides his arm around my waist. "I love you," he mouths.

He gets it.

"Who knew that the ugliest furniture in all of the land would be so exciting," he whispers.

I elbow him in the ribs. "Hush up."

"Do you want it all delivered?" the cashier asks. "Or take some now?"

"Umm." I look at all our things. "We'll take the lamps with us and the board games if that's okay."

Eddie nods. "Yes good idea, Hazen, so they don't get broken," he whispers.

We load up our arms and make our way out to the car. "Now to the rug store," Christopher announces. "And we need new blankets and some kitchen things, saucepans, and cooking shit. I'm going to learn how to cook if it kills me."

"That's if it doesn't kill us first," I reply.

Eddie's shoulders hunch up in excitement and I pull him into a hug, he's so excited he can hardly stand still.

"We better hurry before the shops close, then. We have lots of things to get," I tell them, we load our things into the car and I smile goofily through the windscreen.

Making a home with my boys.

This is a happy day.

———

"The truck's here," Eddie calls from his waiting place on the front veranda.

"Already?" Christopher gasps. "Why are they so fucking early?"

We've been rushing around to try and get ready for this

furniture arrival since six this morning, we shopped until we dropped yesterday and then got dinner on the way home. By the time we finally walked in the door it was after 9 p.m. and we fell into bed exhausted.

There are boxes and rugs and new kitchen crap everywhere.

"Hello," we hear Eddie call to the delivery driver.

"You better go out there."

"I'm unrolling the rugs like you told me to," Christopher grunts. "Pick a job, Hayden, because there is only one of me. Contrary to what you may think I'm not a magician you know?"

"Someone's snarky today." I smirk.

"Busy. The word is busy," he huffs as he marches outside. "I notice your rugs aren't rolled out yet."

"Hello," he calls as he opens the screen door.

"Where do you want it?" the guy calls.

"Inside, please."

"Is that the biggest door?"

Christopher pauses as if not knowing what they mean.

"Yes," I call.

"Yes," he and Eddie call in unison.

The delivery men begin to carry the furniture inside as I direct them where to put things. Both couches in the living area and an armchair, the other couch and two armchairs in the formal living room and then the spectacular dining table into its position in the dining room.

As each piece goes in I feel a little more of the heart of the home click into place, as if it's been waiting for exactly that chair to come back to life. The place is cozy and eclectic and everything is coming together just perfectly.

"You guys own a florist shop?" one of the delivery drivers asks.

Christopher and I frown, not understanding what he means.

"Oh no, that's him being romantic." Eddie points to Christopher with his thumb. "Nearly killed himself with pollen too. Had a sneezing attack and all."

The removalist frowns and then walks back outside without saying a word.

"Stop telling people our shit," Christopher whispers angrily to Eddie. "That information is on a need-to-know basis only."

"But you did nearly die from pollen," Eddie fires back.

"You're about to die in a moment, overshare that."

The men struggle through the front door with the last of the furniture, the purple armchair. "Where do you want this?"

"Upstairs." Eddie beams. "In my room." He takes the stairs two at a time and emotion overwhelms me.

Christopher frowns in question.

"Did you hear him, *in my room*."

Christopher pulls me into a hug and kisses my forehead. "Sounds pretty good, huh?"

"The best."

————

"Come on, get in the car," I call.

"Where are we going?" Christopher asks.

"We have to go and meet the neighbors."

He looks at me blankly. "Why?"

"Because that's what you do." I roll my eyes. Seriously, where is this man from?

"But I don't want to meet the neighbors."

"Why? Because they would judge you because you don't want to meet the neighbors?"

"You're overbearing sometimes, you know that?"

I smile sweetly. "I do actually."

It's day five of living in heaven and Christopher is getting into the swing of never wanting to leave, he struggled going to get milk this morning.

I walk back in through the front door. "Eddie," I call. "Come on, we're going for a drive."

"Okay." He comes bounding down the stairs. "Where are we going?"

"To meet the neighbors," Christopher replies dryly. "I don't even like fucking neighbors."

"Will you stop swearing all the time?" I snap.

"Stop giving me things to swear about then."

"Get in the fucking car."

"I thought you said we couldn't swear?"

"Christopher..." I widen my eyes; I swear to god he's like an annoying five-year-old.

"Fine."

We all pile into the car and head off down the long winding driveway while I smile goofily out the window and look at the green rolling hills. "This driveway is the most beautiful driveway in all of the land."

"You told us that already."

"Something tells me that she's going to tell us that every time we drive down it," Eddie replies casually from the back seat.

We get to the end of the driveway and Christopher turns to look at me. "I don't even know where the neighbors are."

"Turn right," I direct him.

"What if they're left?"

"We're going left too in a minute, just drive."

Christopher's eyes meet Eddie's in the rearview vision mirror. "Don't get any ideas, kid, this is not going be one of those weird, inbred places where we're friends with the neighbors and hang out on Saturday nights toasting marshmallows and shit."

I smirk. "It might be."

"Hayden." He looks over at me. "I've done a lot of shit that isn't my normal jam but I draw the line at being fake farming friends with people."

"Just a quick introduction, that's all. Don't get ahead of yourself, Christopher. They probably won't even like you."

"What does that mean?" He frowns over at me.

"Well...you're you."

His mouth falls open in horror. "And what is wrong with being me?" he gasps in outrage.

"Nothing." *Jeez.* "It was a joke, stop being so touchy."

"For your information, they will fucking love me."

We get to the next driveway and Christopher puts his blinker on and turns in. The driveway isn't as long as ours, the house is closer to the road, we drive through paddock after paddock of beautiful cattle and I look around in awe.

"Oh, he's got good stock."

"Bet you want to wank those cows," Christopher mutters dryly.

"No actually, I don't."

"Why not?"

"Because you don't wank cows, you wank bulls."

"Semantics."

"Not really, they don't have dicks."

Christopher's eyes meet Eddie's in the rearview mirror once more. "Seriously, are you hearing the shit that I have to put up with here?"

Eddie's smile is so big that he's nearly splitting his face.

We get to the house and pull in, it's old and decrepit and looks like it needs a good lick of paint. A woman comes out the front door when she hears us pull up.

"Hello," I call.

"Hello." She smiles. "Can I help you?"

Christopher looks like he just swallowed a fly, this is so far out of his comfort zone.

"We moved in next door last weekend and I wanted to come over and meet you."

"Oh…" She smiles. "Come in, come in. Keith," she calls, "our new neighbors are here to meet us."

The screen door opens and an old burly man comes into view. "Hello." He smiles, he has a kind face and weathered hands.

"Hello, I'm Christopher Miles." Christopher shakes his hand. "This is Eddie, and this is Hayden, my fiancée."

Fiancée.

Hearing that will never grow old.

"Hello, I'm Keith, and this is my wife, Jane."

"Hello."

"You've got some beautiful cattle there, Keith," I smile.

"Sure do. Got the prizewinning bull down there, won the show three years in a row."

"Oh my gosh, really."

I can't look at Christopher because I know how badly he wants to roll his eyes right now.

"Yep. Don't we, Janey?"

Jane smiles warmly, it's obvious she's very proud of her husband and their cows.

"Hayden wanks bulls," Christopher interrupts us.

My god.

Keith's and Jane's faces fall.

"I'm into animal husbandry."

"Well, well." Keith seems excited. "That's a very interesting field, that is."

"My parents own a huge cattle farm and hopefully one day our farm next door will have some cattle on it too." I smile hopefully.

"Well, you need to go to the cattle auctions next Tuesday. It's only on three times a year."

"There's auctions next Tuesday?" I ask, excited.

"Best thoroughbreds in the land will be on sale."

From the corner of my eye I see something coming down the front steps toward us and I glance up to see the cutest brown puppy of all time.

"Oh..." Eddie gasps as he bends to pat it.

"You want one?"

Eddie's eyes flick to me.

"Absolutely not," Christopher cuts in.

"They'll go quick, their father is the best working dog I've ever had."

"Working dogs," I whisper. "I do need a working dog."

"Come around the house and I'll show you."

Eddie and I follow her around and out the back to a barn and there's puppies everywhere, brown kelpies, cute as a button.

"Oh my gosh." I bend down as the puppies run around in circles and jump up and nip us.

One grabs Christopher's jeans with his teeth. "Don't." He subtly tries to push one away with his foot.

Eddie is sitting down on the ground, puppies all over him, and I smile as I watch on.

"Good working dogs, you say?" I ask again.

"The best you'll ever get." Keith replies.

"How much are you selling them for?"

"Hayden..." Christopher taps me on the back.

"I normally sell them for five hundred each, but seeing you're our neighbor, I'll give you two for the price of one," Keith continues.

Christopher taps me on the back, harder now. "Hayden, a word...in private."

"Just a minute, Keith." I hold my finger up and step to the side. "What is it?" I ask Christopher.

"We can't have a dog from here," he whispers. "It's not happening."

Eddie comes and stands next to us as he listens in.

"You said I could do whatever I wanted at the farm," I reply.

"Key word farm," he whispers. "It's not a fucking zoo."

"I told you that I need working dogs. I'm not sure if you realize this, but a farm is not a farm without animals."

"You don't have cows yet, where are you going to work the dogs, in the kitchen? Newsflash, Hayden, they don't cook."

"We need dogs," I tell him.

Eddie's eyes widen in excitement as he looks up at Christopher all hopeful like.

"Don't gang up on me. All I'm saying is, you need a pedigree and I think you should look into this further, you don't just buy the first brown dogs you see next door because they are cute," he whispers angrily as he looks between us.

"Best guard dogs too," Keith adds.

Christopher's ears prick up. "Guard dogs? Are they vicious?"

"No, but they'll let you know the minute someone is on your land, very protective over their family."

Christopher's eyes hold his and I know he's piqued his interest now. "What about wolves, do they kill wolves?"

Keith throws his head back and laughs out loud. "You're hilarious, man."

Or just plain stupid.

"You won't even know they're there; Eddie and I will look after them, won't we, Eddie?" I say.

Eddie bounces on the spot. "Yes. I promise," he stammers, barely able to get the words out through his excitement.

Christopher fakes a smile.

I giggle. "He's a bit too citified, Keith. This is his first farm and we've got to train him up."

"I am not citified." Christopher gasps, indignant.

I hold my fingers up to symbolize a pinch. "Little bit."

"Okay Eddie, pick two, one boy and one girl." I smile.

Eddie's eyes widen with excitement. "Are you serious?"

"Aha."

Eddie drops to his knee and gets to work playing with the pups, while he works out which ones he wants. "This one's a girl." I point to the little one in the corner.

"No, she's too timid, she won't be a good worker," says Keith. "Get the naughty ones, they're the best."

"Timid works for me," Christopher whispers with an elbow.

"Come, I'll show you something else," Jane smiles to me.

She takes me around the corner into another set of sheds.

"Look at these ones." She opens the door and there are kittens as far as you can see, there must be twenty.

"We had two girls get pregnant before they could get desexed, you can have these for free."

My eyes widen. Kittens. Christopher really is going to go postal.

His words come back to me: This is your farm, you can do whatever you want to run it and make it feel like home.

"Okay, I'll take two." I smile. "Another boy and a girl."

"Which ones do you want, love?"

I look them over, they're all pretty similar. The two mothers are sisters, gray and black, there's a few tortoise-shells and one ginger.

"I'll have the ginger, if he's a boy."

"Yes, I think so, let me check."

"And the girls, are they ready to go now?"

"Yes, nine weeks old, we really want them to go to a good home. I would be grateful if you take them."

"Okay, how about this little gray one here." I pick it up and turn it over, oh, it's another boy. I put him back down.

A little darker gray one comes over to me and I pick it up and roll it over. "This is a girl."

"Yeah, she's cute, that one, real mischievous."

"I like her already, we'll take this one too."

"Let me put them in a box for you, I'll go inside and get one," says Jane. She disappears inside and I walk back out to find Christopher and Eddie on their knees surrounded in puppies.

"Do these dogs eat shoes?" Christopher asks.

"If you leave them out they will," Keith replies dryly.

Christopher twists his lips, unimpressed.

"Do they eat much?"

"They will eat whatever you give them." Keith frowns over at Christopher. "You've never had a dog before?"

Christopher straightens his shirt as if annoyed. "I come from New York, we didn't have animals growing up."

"What the hell did you move out here for, then?"

I roll my lips to hide my smile, Christopher must be asking himself the same question. "I fell in love with a country girl and I'm trying to make her happy so I'm learning how to be a farmer now."

Keith smiles and then chuckles. "You got a big learning curve coming for you, boy, especially if she's a cowgirl."

Christopher stays silent as the puppies circle him "I kind of like this little one with sticking-up ears," he says.

"That's a girl."

"Which one do you like, Eddie?" I ask.

"I like this little one here." There's a little puppy chewing on his hand.

"Is that a boy?" He turns it round. "Yep, looks like it."

"So shall we take those two?" I ask.

Christopher drags his hand down his face and I can see that he's regretting this already. "I guess."

Eddie is beside himself and almost skips back to the car holding his two puppies.

Me too, I can hardly contain my excitement.

"I'll have to drop the money back to you, Keith, I don't have my wallet with me."

"That's alright, love, whenever you get to it."

We head back out toward the car and see Jane standing waiting with the box. "Here you go, love, they will need their injections, they've only had their first ones."

"Thanks, Jane." I take the box from her.

Christopher's eyes hold mine. "What's in the box?"

"Kittens."

His eyes widen. "As in plural?"

"As in two."

"I know what cats do in houses and gym bags, Hayden. I did not sign up for this."

Keith and Jane laugh and so do I.

Christopher fakes a smile and I know he's literally on the verge of a mental breakdown. We climb into the car and put the puppies in the back seat with Eddie. The two kittens are in the box in the front on my lap. "Nice to meet you." Keith smiles.

"I wish I could say the same thing," Christopher mutters under his breath.

I giggle, this is truly hilarious.

The car is silent as we drive down the driveway and I know Christopher is holding his tongue with all of his might, he glances over at me. "Was this your plan all along?" he asks.

Totally.

"What do you mean?" I act innocent.

"Do you mind telling me how on earth we go to meet the neighbors and come home with two dogs and two cats?"

"Farms need animals."

"Cows, Hayden, they need cows."

"Trust me, they need cats and dogs too."

He rolls his eyes.

"Do you want a mice and rat plague, Christopher?"

He glances over at me.

"Yeah that's right, mice and rats have lice and lice get under your skin and eat you from the inside out."

"Is that a joke?" he gasps, horrified.

"No, I'm deadly serious. Once you have a lice plague in your home you cannot get rid of them. You have to literally burn the house down to kill them. Cats keep rodents and pests under control, they are the epicenter for a clean and well-kept farm."

"Well why did you only get two? We should have got four of the fuckers,"

Eddie starts to giggle in the back seat and I turn around to see the two puppies jumping up licking his face, killing him with kindness. "I think he likes you, baby." I smile.

Christopher's eyes rise to the rearview mirror and he smirks, even he can't deny how fun this is. "Relax, dog, you start your wolf kill training as soon as we get home."

"Who's going to train him?" I ask.

Christopher widens his eyes. "Hayden Whitmore."

———

"So what do I say again?" Christopher asks.

"Say that you need five rolls of chicken wire with the largest thread that they have."

"But why do I need chicken wire when it's for dog fences?"

"It's just called chicken wire but it's not just for chickens."

Christopher rolls his eyes. "Who is in charge of marketing for this wire company? It's obvious that they have no idea what they are fucking doing." He continues to walk out to the car and opens the door. "What do we need this for again?"

"To make some temporary safe areas for the puppies to play in outside until they are older. They can't just roam free; they are too little and will get lost."

"Are you sure?" He frowns. "That doesn't sound right to me."

I raise my eyebrow. "What do you think happens?"

"I don't know." He shrugs. "Let them roam free and sniff shit out, guard-dog style."

"They are little baby puppies."

"My point exactly, they don't want to be kept in chicken wire. It's emasculating."

"They can't be left alone this early."

"But we are just inside."

"Christopher! Just fucking do it," I snap as I lose the last of my patience.

He rolls his eyes and gets into the car. "I'm going now."

"Good." I cross my arms. "About time."

"And I might come home with all sorts of shit from the hardware store." He grabs his crotch with a wink. "Hardware."

"Okay."

"Maybe even some more animals." He shrugs casually as if trying to scare me.

"Okay, if they have baby chickens grab me a few."

"What?" He scoffs. "You cannot be serious?"

"Well...you are buying chicken wire."

"Oh for fuck's sake, Hayden. Enough with the animals." He looks up into the house. "Eddie," he calls. "Hurry up."

Eddie comes flying out of the house and bounces into the front seat.

Christopher won't go anywhere without his trusty little apprentice farmer. I smile as I watch them disappear into the distance, I can only imagine the conversations they must have about the errands I send them on.

Christopher

We pull the car to a halt in the crowded parking lot, there are trailers and trucks everywhere. We are at the cattle auctions, I made Elliot come with me.

"Never thought I'd be fucking doing this, that's for sure." Elliot says as he looks around.

"What's that?"

"Buying cows for your fiancée to wank."

I smirk as I turn the car off, "That makes two of us." We get out of the car and walk across the large lawn towards the hall.

"Tell me why we're doing this without Hayden again?"

"I want to surprise her. Up until now she's bought everything but...I," I shrug.

"You what?"

"If I'm honest, I'm kind of loving this farm thing and I want to surprise her with something that I know she will love. Something meaningful."

"Okay, makes sense." He frowns, "I guess." We turn the corner into the hall and stop dead on the spot.

"What the hell is this?" I whisper.

There's a million people, cows are in the centre and the auctioneer is talking so fast that I can't even understand him.

"It's like Times square on fucking crack." Elliot frowns.

"What's the plan?" Elliot asks as he looks around.

"We buy five strong looking male calves and then get the fuck out of here."

"All male?" He frowns.

"Yeah," I shrug, "That's what she needs."

"That's dumb."

"How is that fucking dumb?"

"Think about it, who's going to be hornier? Five boys stuck in a paddock together or three boys who have four hot, big titted chicks in the next paddock to imagine fucking."

I narrow my eyes, "You think we need cow porn?"

"One hundred percent."

"Okay, three boys, four girls." I think for a moment, "Maybe four boys and three girls."

"No, they need variety."

"Okay, four boys and five girls. But they have to be hot girls."

Elliot nods as he looks around, "This will be a piece of cake, if anyone knows cows it's us."

"Why do you say that?"

"We've both fucked a lot of cows in our day."

I smirk and then chuckle, "This is true."

Three months later.

"No, no, listen to me and concentrate. This way here..." the teacher, Mr. Enid, points to a piece of paper with his pen, "...goes over to this one here, remember like we did the other day?"

Eddie sits back in his chair at the dining table, deflated. *I feel sick to my stomach.*

This hard to watch, Eddie is struggling with his reading and writing lessons and we don't know how to help him.

It's like everything is on hold in his life until we can get this under his belt and achieved. He can't even work at McDonald's unless he can read and write.

He loves the farm and is so happy working with

Hayden, and he needs this family time, we know he does. But in the back of our minds we also know that he is destined for more, and he needs to conquer this reading and writing thing to accomplish what is meant for him.

"Let's go back over that again, Eddie, and I want you to concentrate this time."

"He is concentrating," I snap.

The teacher looks up. "With all due respect, Mr. Miles, you can't interrupt my classes. Eduardo needs to try harder."

"That is all for today." I cut him off.

Eddie smiles up at me and I can see the relief written all over his face.

"In fact." I pause as I contemplate our options, Hayden wanted to fire him a week ago and I talked her out of it, I came home from work today early to specifically sit in on the lesson. Hayden is right, this isn't working. "We won't be needing your services any longer. Your teaching style isn't working for Eddie."

Eddie bites his bottom lip to stifle his smile.

"Please send us an account of all that we owe you."

"You're making a mistake," Mr. Enid replies.

"I disagree. Good luck with everything." I shake his hand and direct for Eddie to do the same. "Thank you," Eddie says with the best of manners.

Eddie and I watch on as Mr. Enid walks out and gets into his car, and I turn to Eddie. "What a tool."

Eddie smirks. "Maybe."

———

I stand at the window and stare out over the London skyline, my mind is miles away, it's with Eddie at home.

"What's wrong with you? You look like you just have the world on your shoulders." Elliot asks from behind me.

"I've got a lot on my mind," I sigh.

"Such as?"

"I don't know if I've done the right thing with Eddie, maybe I should have put him into school. He is struggling with this language barrier and I don't know how to make it any better for him."

"I thought you had him a tutor?"

"I do...did, he came to the house four times a week. But he's...everything seems to be like really hard and I know just how intelligent he is, I don't understand why he's struggling so much. The thing is, he's never read or written in any language so to add to it a new language is another level of hardship. Maybe we should put him in school?"

"What is the thought process behind not doing that?" Elliot frowns.

"Hayden wants him to feel secure and safe within himself before he is put into social situations with mean kids. She thinks he's going to snap if they push him."

"Good point. Can we find him a job here?"

"This is the problem; he can't even work in the mail room if he can't read or write. This really is a major road-block in his life right now and I need to find a way to help and motivate him. I just don't know how."

Elliot thinks for a minute. "You need to think like a fourteen-year-old boy."

I frown. "What do you mean?"

"What would have motivated you when you were fourteen?"

I think for a moment, a new plan comes into mind and I smirk. "That's it." I slap him hard on the back. "That's fucking it."

Elliot chuckles. "Are you thinking what I'm thinking?"

"You bet I am."

———

I drive up the long winding driveway toward our house and I catch sight of something magnificent in the field, I pull the car to a stop as I stare on in awe.

The sun is slowly setting over the mountain, the meadows are dancing with colors of gold. Eddie is driving the tractor and Hayden is sitting up on the back behind him with the two puppies. They are laughing and talking and having the absolute time of their lives. Every now and then the puppies will bark and Hayden and Eddie roar in laughter at what must be the funniest joke of all time.

They don't see me, but every cell in my body sees them.

I can feel the happiness as it oozes from their souls.

This farm, these people, this life.

It's perfect, where the three of us belong.

Together.

I couldn't ask for a happier place to live...for Eddie to call home.

I know it's not Spain and I know we have so many more hurdles to cross but between the three of us, there is so much love.

I watch them until they disappear over the hill, they still haven't seen me and probably won't be back to the house for hours. This is what they do here, disappear into god knows where.

I make my way up to the house and walk in to see Sylvester and Minnie, our cats, lying in front of the fire, stretched out and sleeping like logs.

I stare at them all relaxed like. "Dare I ask if you two wild beasts caught any mouses today?"

I frown as I mouth the word.

Mouses.

"Mice, did you two catch any mice today?"

They keep sleeping.

"Everybody is working in this house to keep the wheels running except you two," I tell them as I kick off my shoes and take off my jacket. "You better start pulling your weight around here or that's it. No more fire and no more free meals."

I drop a cushion off the couch onto the floor beside them.

"Because if we get lice and we have to burn the house down then I'm leaving you two inside it." I lie down on the floor beside them in front of the fire with my head on the cushion.

Sylvester looks up as if just realizing I'm home and gets up and walks over and sits on me. "I'm not a chair you know?" I tell him.

I scratch his chin and he purrs and closes his eyes, relaxed and living the life of a king.

It brings a smile to my face; these cats couldn't catch a mouse if their lives depended on it.

"Maybe you'll have to start cooking instead."

Hayden

Knock, knock, sounds at the door.

Eddie's new tutor is here, I bound down the stairs and stop on the spot when I see who is at the door.

A Spanish bombshell, curvy and gorgeous and in her late twenties, she's wearing a long black pencil skirt and tight-fitting sweater blouse, her long dark hair is out and full and she has a real Sofía Vergara vibe.

A walking sex bomb.

"Hello, my name is Lucia. I'm here to see Eddie. I'm his new teacher."

I stare at her, shocked to my core...

What are you going to teach him?

Eddie's eyes widen as he stares at her. "I'm...I 'm...I'm... Eddie," he stammers as he points to his chest.

I roll my lips to hide my smile at his reaction to her.

Christopher Miles...you snake.

"Come in." I smile.

"Do you...do you want a drink or something?" Eddie offers her at a million miles per minute.

"That would be lovely. Thank you, Eduardo." She smiles calmly, it's obvious that every male she meets would have this reaction to her.

Eddie smiles goofily up at her and then his eyes flick to me to make sure I'm seeing this too.

Diabolical.

"Let's just get to know each other today, Eddie," she says. "Maybe you could show me around your farm."

Eddie's eyes widen with excitement. "Su...sure," he gasps, his eyes flick to me and then back to her and then back to me, he's so excited that he doesn't know where to look.

Over the next two hours I watch on as Eddie hangs off every word that comes out of Lucia's mouth. He took her for a drive on the tractor and has been explaining everything about our farm and animals to her in great detail. Which I'm really pleased about because she can now see how switched on he is.

She's kind and thoughtful and he is already so much more engaged than he was with his last teacher.

"I'll see you tomorrow, Eddie?" she asks.

He smiles goofily. "Okay."

"Your father wants us to do this every day."

Eddie's eyes widen in excitement. "Sounds so great," he gasps. "Really, really great."

I bet it does...you little demon, you.

He walks out the front to wave her off and I watch them through the window. Eddie is glowing with excitement and I have to admit, I'm even excited for him.

Later that night I hear Christopher's car pull up the driveway and I walk out to meet him.

"Hi there," he says as he gets out of his car, he takes me into his arms and kisses me softly, his tongue gently brushing against mine.

"Tell me you did not do that on purpose." I smirk up at him.

He gives me a sexy wink. "Whatever it takes."

The Wedding

The farm is abuzz with catering staff, florists and bartenders.

People are carrying tables; marquee white tents are being erected and flowers are everywhere. Preparation for our wedding tomorrow at my parents' farm in Finger Lakes in the US is in full swing.

I wanted to get married here, it was important to my parents and important to me. This farm is the very essence of my soul, marrying my soulmate could only ever be done here.

Christopher really wanted to get married at our farm but he conceded once he knew how much it meant to me.

Eddie and I have been here for a week already and Christopher flew in on Wednesday after work.

On Monday, Christopher and I go on our honeymoon to the Maldives and Mom and Dad and Eddie will return to our farm in the UK, we have too much going on there at the moment for it to be left alone for more than a few days.

The good news is that Mom and Dad have a full-time caretaker here now, so they are free to travel whenever they want. Eddie has become very close to my parents; my father especially has taken him in under his wing and I'm quite sure that they come and stay at our farm for extended times now to see Eddie and not us.

The Miles family have all arrived and are staying at a hotel in town, we are having a big pre-wedding dinner tonight here with just the two families.

I always get nervous when our families come together, they are just so different and my dad can be so abrasive and blunt. Everyone seems to walk around on their tiptoes so that they don't rock the boat.

Tristan's boys are always a great icebreaker though, they seem to fit in wherever they are and as more and more babies arrive things are getting busier and more hectic. Eddie is still quiet around the extended family; he will get there; I know he will. It's just that every time we come together there is so much going on that he just stays quiet and tries to blend in. I can't wait for the day that they get to know and love him the way that we do.

"Okay, babe." Christopher kisses me softly, his hands on my behind. "I'm going to go. I'll be back in a few hours."

"Okay." I kiss him again, our lips lingering over each other's.

Christopher is going to have a drink with his brothers before our dinner tonight. As close as ever, any chance they get to spend time together they take it. The four of them went to Vegas last month for his bachelor party and I don't know what they did there but Christopher slept for three days once he got home. His voice was so hoarse from laughing and drinking that I hate to even imagine what went on.

"Tomorrow." He smiles against my lips, bringing me back to the here and now.

"Tomorrow…" My heart swells, he kisses me softly again as he grips my hair in both his hands.

"God, I can't fucking wait until you're my wife."

I smile against his lips; we are so in love.

The life that we are building together is more than either of us could have ever imagined. Eddie being a part of our lives is such a gift, he is such a special person. The kindest, most thoughtful human I have ever met.

Funny and intelligent, witty and smart. Hardworking too, the best we have on the farm, he's up looking after the animals first in the morning and he's the last to check on them every night.

In amongst the chaos and the adoration of our dogs and cats and cows, he's found himself, he's our king. The glue that holds us all together.

I'm not sure if the corporate Miles world will ever be for

him. Christopher seems to think that this is his grounding stage where the farm is everything to him, it's his home that he's helping to build. But he thinks eventually Eddie will need more and then will come to work for Miles Media.

Me...I'm not so sure.

I think back to him bartending in the backpackers and what his life would have turned out like if we never met and I can't imagine it. It seems so removed from the life we live now.

He would have been fine and he would have excelled in whatever he did, he has that deep kind of resilience that can't be taught. But I'm so glad that he doesn't have to be anymore. He can be soft and vulnerable and just loved for who he is.

He can choose whatever path in life that he wants to.

"Don't get drunk," I remind Christopher. "We have the dinner tonight, remember?"

"I know."

"Yeah, you always say you know, but whenever you get with your brothers something snaps in your brain."

He smirks. "Because they are fucking alcoholics, that's why. They peer group pressure me."

I giggle. "Sure they do, you're the worst out of all of them."

"See you in a few hours." I watch him get into his old beat-up truck and pull out down the driveway, I smile as he disappears. So much has changed, I remember the first time he came here and was so mortified by the red utility I made him hire. Now he prefers the older beat-up cars, he reckons they make him feel tougher.

I don't know who he is kidding, he could never be tough on the land.

Even our cats boss him around, he's the softy with the huge heart.

I hear a sound in the distance and look over to see Eddie on the tractor following my father down to the far paddock.

Where are they going now?

"There is no time to fix fences today, boys, we have a wedding to organize."

I walk into the house, take the stairs, unzip the garment bag as it hangs on the back of the door and stare lovingly at the most beautiful wedding dress I have ever seen.

My heart skips a beat.

I'm getting married tomorrow.

Christopher

We all hold our drinks together for a toast. "To Hayden." Jameson smiles.

"To Hayden," we all repeat.

"Can you believe it?" I smirk. "How the fuck did I talk her into marrying me, I will never know."

"Me neither," Tristan agrees. "Poor bitch should run while she can."

Elliot chuckles. "Just hurry up and get the ring on so she can't back out."

We collectively take a sip of our customary Blue Label scotch. "This is a weird day, isn't it?" I ask them.

"How so?"

"Well, I'm the last of us to get married."

"The end of an era." Jameson nods, almost sadly.

"It is," we all agree as we fall pensive.

"And not one of us married the kind of girl we thought we would," Tristan replies.

"I did." Elliot smiles wistfully. "I married my dream girl."

Jameson rolls his eyes. "You're fucking pathetic, you know that? You didn't even know she painted those paintings."

"But she did." Elliot smirks as he holds up his glass in a toast. "But she did. Her art was in my heart."

They all groan in disgust.

"Like I said, pathetic." Jameson curls his lip. "And for the record, if Harvey calls me boy tonight, I'm knocking him out," he adds.

Tristan chuckles. "Please do, I would pay good money to see him kick your ass."

"I'd like to see that," I reply. "He could kill you with his eyes closed."

"Don't doubt it," Elliot agrees. "He is one tough motherfucker."

"So what's next for the Miles brothers?" Elliot asks. "What happens from here?"

"We watch our kids grow up and take over," Jameson replies with a shrug.

"Miles, the Next Generation." I smile sadly. "The end of an era." I put my hand over my heart. "Don't, it's making me sad. I don't want our stories to be over, I want to stay here forever."

Jameson fills our glasses again.

"I'm not allowed to get drunk," I say. "I've been warned."

"Fuck off." He fills my glass to the top. "You're not married yet." He raises his glass for another toast. We all smile, his toasts have always been legendary and as we get older we somehow appreciate them more, we put our glasses up to his.

"To the next generation of Miles's, may they live greater, faster, harder, and fuck like demons."

Tristan snorts his drink up his nose. "And for my girls to be virgins forever so that I don't have to kill anybody."

"That too." Elliot nods.

We all chuckle as we toast the closing of an era and the opening of another, to hopes and dreams and fantasies coming true.

"To the next generation of Miles's."

Hayden

We sit out in the garden under a canopy of fairy lights, music is playing and we are all relaxing and on the wind-down for the big day tomorrow, the dinner has been perfect. Great food, great company, wonderful families coming together.

Unsurprisingly, the boys were tipsier than they'd promised to be, hilarious as usual, I swear when these four get together they grow another brain. Sarcasm and wit is their only language.

Dessert has been served and I walk around and collect some plates.

Laughter is loud as all the kids chatter and talk between themselves.

Eddie is quiet and standing back, I'm not sure if something has happened to upset him, but he's not acting like himself.

He helps me collect some plates and my father does too and we walk them up to the catering staff in the kitchen.

Harry is in the kitchen getting a drink.

"Hello, boy," my dad says.

Harry looks at my father deadpan. "Don't call me that."

Eddie's back straightens.

"You're very entitled for a kid," my dad growls.

Oh fuck.

"Outside, everybody." I fake a smile. *Please don't poke the bear, Harry.*

The night has been perfect, don't ruin it.

"I am not entitled," Harry spits angrily. "And I don't appreciate your tone, Harvey."

Oh crap.

"Who's got the tone, boy?" my father sneers.

"I said don't call me that," he fires back. "Are you deaf?"

Jeez, this kid. He's so headstrong, they really do have their hands full with him.

Eddie steps in front of my father, "Don't speak to him like that." He pokes Harrison in the chest. "Apologize." He pokes him again. "Now."

Harry pokes him back. "No. I did nothing wrong. I don't want to be called that, so I won't be."

"You disrespect him and you disrespect me. Apologize. Now." Eddie pushes Harrison on the chest and he stumbles back.

Shit.

"Stop it, boys," I snap, I turn to Patrick. "Go get your father and Christopher."

Patrick looks at me wide eyed, unsure what to do.

"Now,"

Harry pushes Eddie again and Patrick runs outside in search of backup.

"Cut it out, you two," my father growls.

Eddie grabs Harrison by the shirt. "You apologize to Harvey now...or you're going to get it."

"What are you going to do about it, wimp," Harrison fires back. "You can't fight for shit."

My dad throws his head back and laughs out loud, he thinks this is hilarious.

"Stop it," I cry. "Dad, this isn't funny."

The boys grab each other in a headlock and begin to wrestle.

"Argh, what are you doing?" I whisper angrily as I try to pull them apart. "Stop it."

Eddie pushes Harrison toward the front door. "Get out the front, I'm kicking your ass."

"Bring it, pretty boy," Harrison spits. "I'm kicking your fucking ass."

They push each other to the front door as I run to the back door. "Christopher," I call.

Fuck, where is he?

Claire sees my face and instantly stands.

Everyone looks up from their tables to see what the commotion is about.

"What's happening?" Claire whispers.

"Harrison and Eddie are fighting."

"What?" Her eyes widen. "Where?"

"Out the front."

We both go running through the house and burst out the front door to see Eddie and Harrison rolling around on the ground fighting in the dark.

"Ahh, Harry," Claire cries. "Stop it."

Eddie has Harry's face munched into the ground. "Apologize," he yells.

"Go to hell," Harry spits as he tastes the dirt.

Tristan and Christopher come running around the side of

the house. "What the fuck is going on?" Tristan yells, he pulls Eddie off Harrison and throws him backward.

"He started it," Harrison yells.

"Apologize, you coward," Eddie yells. "You apologize right this minute or I'm kicking your ass again."

Christopher's and my eyes are wide, we've never seen this side of Eddie.

"What happened?" Tristan glares at Harrison, "What do you need to apologize for?"

Harrison shrugs. "I don't want to be called boy. I'm not taking that shit."

A loud laugh sounds from behind us and we turn to see a very tipsy Jameson thinking this is the funniest thing he's ever seen. "Fight, fight, fight," he chants as he shadow-punches the air.

Tristan breaks into a broad smile when he sees him. "Fuck off, idiot."

"Apologize to Harvey, right now," Eddie demands.

Harry narrows his eyes as he glares at Eddie. "Sorry."

"Sorry for what?" Eddie barks.

Harrison exhales heavily. "Sorry for being rude, Harvey."

As if his work is done, Eddie dusts his hands and his shirt off and walks inside, Harrison follows and Tristan takes off after them, not trusting that the fight is actually over.

Claire, Christopher and I stand shell shocked, "I have never seen Eddie like that." I murmur. "I'm so sorry, he was out of line. It's not his place to pull up Harry."

"Harry is a little piece of work. He probably deserved it," Claire whispers. "It's me who is sorry." She takes off into the house and my father smiles and then chuckles. "This is great," he laughs.

"This is not great, Dad?" I gasp. "I've never seen that side of him."

"How do you think Eddie survived on his own for so long?" he asks.

Christopher and I stare at him, lost for words.

"He doesn't take shit from anyone, and finally, he's bringing that over to his new life. It's about time he demanded their respect."

Christopher drags his hands through his hair. "Fuck."

We walk inside to see a very sheepish Harrison and Eddie sitting on the couch with Tristan in between them.

Jameson and Elliot are fake punching each other as they put on a show for the living room. Everyone is acting serious but the two drunken idiots are actually quite amusing.

Eddie's eyes rise to meet Christopher's and Christopher winks at him, Eddie's shoulders relax a little, knowing it's going to be okay.

I inwardly smile, I think Dad might be right.

Eddie demanded their respect tonight; he's finally broken through the barrier in his new life of asking for what he knows he deserves.

I can't be angry for that.

How could I be?

Go, baby.

———

"This is it, baby girl." Dad smiles down at me. "You look absolutely breathtaking."

We stand at the end of the flower-strung aisle, the wedding march playing, in front of our friends and family, my veil firmly in place.

My fitted lace dress is the perfect finale to my fairy tale.

Marrying my dream man in my dream dress.

Christopher and Eddie are waiting for me at the other end. Black dinner suits and beaming happy smiles.

With every step we take down the aisle a little more of my destiny clicks into place. My heart free-falling from my chest.

It's him. It's always been him.

Today I am marrying Christopher Miles.

We finally get to the end of the aisle and my father kisses both of my cheeks and I turn toward Christopher.

He kisses me and leans up onto his toes in excitement, his big, beautiful smile on display.

My heart is full.

And as everyone who is dearest to us watches on, I marry the love of my life.

———

The room is hot and steamy, a perspiration sheen covers my skin.

I'm on my hands and knees, the sound of the bed slamming into the wall with force.

"You take my cock like a good fucking wife," Christopher growls as he pulls my head back by my hair, he's standing behind me, his legs spread and thick quads contracting with every pump.

I clench as my body ripples around his large erection.

Holy fuck...

The honeymoon of all honeymoons.

I have well and truly been broken in.

We've been fucking for hours...days.

His hands tighten on my hair as he pulls my head back so

that my eyes meet his. "I'm going to blow in your mouth, Mrs. Miles."

I smile up at him and lick my lips.

Please.

———

We walk up the gangplank hand in hand, "Good afternoon Mr and Mrs Miles." The captain smiles. The staff are lined up in their white and navy uniforms to greet us and I can't help but get a sense of de-ja-vu. It doesn't seem that long ago that we were working in a place just like this.

We are boarding Christophers super Yacht and every single time we do it, it just seems so crazy and surreal.

It's like we have two different lives, the family farm in London with Eddie and then when Eddie stays with my parents, we live a life of the rich and famous.

Yachts and private planes, black tie balls and exotic people and places.

We are in St Tropez in the south of France, we flew over in the private jet and now have a week on the yacht.

Crazy...even to me.

We board and walk into the most beautiful yacht I have ever seen; I take the stairs to our bedroom and look around, through the huge glass windows, I stare out over the view of the marina and Christophers hands snake around me from behind, "Finally.... we're here." He whispers against my cheek. "Let's get busy." His erection digs into my hip.

"We are not getting busy; they're going to be here soon."

"They'll be hours, they're always late."

A shell horn sounds and we glance up and Basil, Bernadette, Bodie and Kimberly are coming up the boardwalk dressed in full cabaret fancy dress, laughing loudly as they chat.

"Fuck me dead." Christopher whispers.

I burst out laughing, the best part about our extravagant holidays is that we get to bring our friends.

Three years later.

I stare at the little girl wrapped tightly in her pink blanket, the perfect blend of Christopher and me.

Evelyn Grace Miles, one week old, and today we get to take her home.

I glance at my watch. "Where are they?"

Christopher and Eddie are coming to pick us up but are running late and I have no idea what they are doing.

So much has changed in our life.

Eddie is now legally our son; we adopted him eighteen months ago and go to Spain for vacation every year. We're hoping to buy a holiday house over there as soon as we get the time to look for one.

As much as we love our time in Spain, Eddie is always the one who is most eager to get back to our farm in the UK. He is totally obsessed with it and says that it's where we belong. He's become quite the competent little farmer.

My mom and dad live in the bottom house of our farm for a few months of the year. One day we hope to get a care-taker to live in one of the houses so that we can go away more often. At the moment we are pretty tied here. I have a herd of the most beautiful cattle in all of the land and my own animal husbandry business. I have two full-time staff to help me with it. I think Eddie is sweet on Melissa, who is one of our trainees. She's a year older than him but they get on well and hang out together. Christopher is watching them like a hawk and has warned Eddie not to touch her or he's dead.

Eddie is reading and writing like a pro and now is going to school as a senior. He is sitting in the top band of his classmates and has lots of friends, he just got his learner license.

Christopher hasn't let me drive with him yet because I was pregnant, all I know is that every time they go driving, Christopher ages about five years and does a cross symbol as he walks into the house as if he is walking into a Catholic church.

The door bursts open and Christopher and Eddie come rushing in. "Sorry we're late," Eddie stammers,

"Hi, Grumps." Christopher kisses me softly; his lips linger on mine.

Having this perfect little version of us has sent Christopher's hormones into overdrive, he cannot love me more.

"You're late." I look between them as I hand Evelyn to Eddie. "Hold your sister." Eddie takes her like a pro and sits down in the chair in the corner of the hospital room, he smiles down at her with so much love.

He's a natural at this big brother thing.

"It was Eddie's fault."

"It was not," Eddie fires back. "You left the gate open and the cows got into the top paddock."

"What?" I frown.

"Then we had to chase them all back in and then I tripped over in cow shit and had to change," Christopher snaps. "Nothing ever runs fucking smooth for us, you know this."

"Don't curse in front of Evelyn," Eddie fires back. "She can hear, you know?"

Christopher punches his fist. "I'm the parent around here."

Eddie rolls his eyes.

"Are my boys ready to take us home?" I ask.

Christopher takes me into his arms and kisses me softly. "You bet we are." He turns to Eddie. "Let me hold her."

"I want to hold her," Eddie replies.

"Later, you're the kid." Christopher takes her from him. "The dad always holds the baby as you leave the hospital, everyone knows that. It's the dad law."

"I'm carrying her into the house when we get home then," Eddie replies.

I roll my eyes. *Fuck my life.* "Are you two going to fight over holding her forever now?"

"Yes," they both say in unison.

Eddie grabs my bags and Christopher puts his arm around his shoulders as he stares lovingly down at our little girl. "Let's take our family home."

Christopher

Five years later.

We sit around the board table, all of us together as we make plans and projections for Miles Media for the next five years.

Tough decisions have to be made, changes bought into place and implemented.

This is the sharp end of the job; it is also where Jameson shines and is at his best.

"Okay." Jameson slides over his folder. "Next. I have

made some recommendations on who I want to train up to management level in the New York office."

I take the folder from him and open it up.

Eduardo Miles

I close the folder and push it back to him, "No."

"What do you mean no?" He frowns.

"He's not ready."

Eddie has been working with Miles Media for three years and I hate to admit it but he's a star in the making.

Sharp and smart with no in between.

Jameson's eyes hold mine across the boardroom table. "I beg to differ."

Tristan and Elliot scoff in disgust.

"Do I look like I'm joking?" I snap. "He is *not* ready."

"You mean...not ready for his overprotective father to let him live his own life and grow into his full potential?" Jameson rolls his eyes. "Give me a break."

I sit back in my chair, annoyed. "I am not being over-protective."

"Yes you are," Tristan replies. "I know how you feel, but you need to let him go."

"You do not know how I feel," I fire back. "You have no fucking idea how I feel."

"Yes. I do. Harrison is also training for management if you didn't remember? He was supposed to come back to Anderson Media straight after his internship and now he won't. Jameson has seduced him into staying."

"Because you work between the two companies," I snap. "You're three days a week at Anderson Media and two days a week at Miles. He doesn't have to choose because his father is involved in both companies."

"That has nothing to do with it," Jameson snaps. "Harrison and Eduardo are needed in New York. They have enough potential, intelligence and grit required for management." He looks between Tristan and me. "You both know that. They are needed in New York. This is their company too; they need to step up and be who we need them to be."

I exhale heavily.

"Eduardo has an inner strength that cannot be taught," Jameson continues. "And when you took him as your son he inherited a privilege. But that privilege comes with duty. And that duty is to Miles Media. I won't have your pansy bullshit excuses that he can't handle it when we all fucking know he could handle more than any of us."

I run my hands through my hair. "Hayden is going to flip, he can't move to New York on his own, he's still too young."

"He's twenty-two," Jameson fires back, "Do you remember what we were all doing at twenty-two? And besides, he won't be on his own, he has Harrison and Fletcher, his two best friends, both living in New York. I'm here and Tristan is here, we can keep an eye on him."

I roll my lips. "I don't like this," I sigh.

"You don't have to," Jameson replies.

"He can live in your penthouse," Elliot says.

"Oh and run amok with Harry and Fletch, that's not a disaster waiting to happen at all, is it?" I sit back, annoyed. "Imagine the three of them together out on the town. He won't leave Hayden and his brothers and sisters anyway; I know he won't."

"Why don't we ask him?" Jameson pushes the buzzer, "Can you send Eduardo in, please, Sammia."

"Yes, sir."

A few moments later a knock sounds at the door. "Come in."

Eddie comes into view and smiles. "Hello."

"Take a seat." Jameson smiles.

Eddie sits down as he looks between us and I smile as I have an out-of-body experience. I see the little boy I met in Spain and now the man sitting here in front of me.

So much has changed and yet everything is the same.

He's wearing a tailored designer suit, the best shoes money can buy and a Rolex watch, and not because I bought it for him.

Because he bought it for him.

"Eddie, we are exceptionally proud of you," Jameson says. "You are a shining light in Miles Media's future."

Emotion overwhelms me and my nostrils flare as I try to hold it together.

"You've been a star in our London office but the time has come."

Eddie looks between us in confusion.

"I would like you to work out of the New York office from here on in," Jameson says. "Tristan will be training you in acquisitions management."

His eyes widen and then flick to me.

I twist my lips as I try to hold my tongue.

"Would you like that?" Jameson asks.

Eddie nods. "Very much, sir. Thank you for the opportunity."

"Then it's settled."

"I'll have to speak to Mom first," Eddie replies. "I can't

agree to anything without talking to her and Dad in private first."

Good boy.

I give him a lopsided smile.

"Okay." Jameson nods. "I respect that, but I need an answer tomorrow."

"Thank you so much, Jameson, this is an incredible opportunity, I'm so grateful." He shakes Jameson's hand; his excitement is bubbling out of him, a tangible force. He then goes around the table and shakes Tristan's hand and Elliot's and then pulls me into a hug. "Thanks, Dad."

No.

I want to throw myself on the floor and tantrum. Beg him not to do this. He can't leave us yet, it's too soon. His siblings need him around. Hayden won't survive without her best little friend.

We're not ready.

He bounces out of the boardroom and Jameson smirks over at my horrified face.

"Calm down, you've done your job, Christopher. He's ready for the next stage of his life, to meet his full potential. You and Hayden need to let him go. It's time for little Eddie from Spain to become Eduardo Miles of New York."

I think back to the first time I met Eddie and how enamored with New York he was. How excited he was just to have a cap with the lettering NY.

My heart twists.

This is his every dream come true.

And he's worked so hard for it, first to arrive to work every day, last to leave. Learning to read and write, completing college, you name it, he's conquered it, without a single complaint.

The bravest person I know.

I've never been so proud of anyone or anything in my life. Hayden and I have had the privilege of loving him and calling him our son.

But becoming Eduardo Miles of New York has always been his destiny, this is his calling.

He will be a force to be reckoned with.

How could we ever stand in the way of an opportunity like this? Through tears in my eyes, I nod as I concede defeat.

"Look after him for me," I whisper.

Jameson shakes my hand. "I promise."

Hayden

Ten years to the day.

The moonlight bounces off the sea, a cool breeze tickles my skin.

Midnight, the witching hour.

I stand on the edge of the beach, my eyes roaming over the sand.

Ten years ago I promised a man that I would meet him on this very beach in Barcelona at midnight.

He tried to kiss me then and I declined, then he told me he was going to steal me from my husband.

I catch sight of his silhouette down by the water's edge and I make my way down to him.

I'm wearing the same bikini I travelled with and my white dress that he loved so much. I kept it especially for this date, to reminisce with a full visual.

Take a step back in time.

Eddie is back at our holiday house here in Spain with his four younger brothers and sisters, two girls and two boys; Evelyn, Mason, Ethan and Aleena.

I'm on the beach meeting the man of dreams.

The one that didn't get away.

Christopher turns, and as he sees me he gives me a breathtakingly beautiful smile; his dark hair is messed up. He's wearing a white linen shirt with the top buttons undone and boardshorts.

But it's his heart that I see.

The blinding beautiful light that shines from within him.

"Hi." I smile as I approach him.

"Hi." He beams, he's holding a flower in his hands, he tucks it behind my ear and then kisses me softly, his lips linger over mine as he holds my face. "You came," he whispers.

I smile against his lips; our story could have been so different.

"Of course I did, you're the love of my life."

He kisses me again. "I'm still going to steal you from your husband."

I giggle. "You'd hate him."

"I heard he's a real fucking wanker.'"

I laugh out loud and he does too as we hold hands and stare at each other.

"Thank you," he whispers.

"For what?"

"For loving me just as I am."

My eyes well with tears and his silhouette blurs.

"For giving me the most wonderful life I could ever have dreamed of."

He kisses me and it's so filled with emotion, powerful and full of love.

The perfect end to our story, and yet just the beginning.

He takes my hand and begins to wade into the water. "This time, Grumps, I'm doing what I should have done last time."

"What's that?"

"I *am* fucking you in the ocean."

My mouth falls open.

"And I don't give a fuck what your husband says." He bends and whips my bikini bottoms off and throws them into the darkness. "Be gone," he yells.

I laugh out loud. "Don't throw them away, how the hell am I going to get out?"

He picks me up and hurls me into the air. "Who fucking cares, we'll stay in here forever."

The End.

Thank you so much for reading and loving The Miles High series.
It's been a dream come true.
Until next time.
Tee xx

Made in United States
Orlando, FL
11 March 2025

59379746R00129